DATE DUE

In the Heart

of the

Valley of Love

Also by Cynthia Kadohata

The Floating World

The Glass Mountains

R

Cynthia Kadohata

In the Heart

of the

Valley of Love

UNIVERSITY OF CALIFORNIA PRESS

Berkeley • Los Angeles • London

Riverside Community College
Library
MAY 00 4800 Magnolia Avenue
Riverside, CA 92506

PS 3561 .A3615 I5 1997

Kadohata, Cynthia.

In the heart of the valley
of love

University of California Press
Berkeley and Los Angeles, California

University of California Press, Ltd.
London, England

First California Paperback Printing 1997

Printed by arrangement with Viking Penguin, a division of Penguin Books USA Inc.

Copyright © Cynthia Kadohata, 1992
All rights reserved

Library of Congress Cataloging-in-Publication Data
Kadohata, Cynthia.
    In the heart of the valley of love / Cynthia Kadohata.
        p.   cm. — (California fiction)
      ISBN 0-520-20728-9 (alk. paper)
       1. Twenty-first century—Fiction. 2. Los Angeles (Calif.)—
Fiction. 3. California—Fiction. I. Title. II. Series.
    PS3561.A3615I5 1997
    813′.54—dc20   96-34569
                                          CIP

Printed in the United States of America
Set in Bodoni Book   Designed by Kate Nichols

1 2 3 4 5 6 7 8 9

The paper used in this publication meets the minimum requirements of American National Standard for Information Sciences—Permanence of Paper for Printed Library Materials, ANSI Z39.48-1984. ∞

Again, for my family

Acknowledgments

The author would like to thank Caitlyn Dlouhy for the generosity of her heart and the sternness of her criticism; Dan Bergner; Deborah Karl; Dawn Seferian, Paul Slovak, and everyone at Viking; the Whiting Foundation and the National Endowment for the Arts; and the incomparable Mark Nine.

Contents

Contents x

In the Heart

of the

Valley of Love

Black Pearls

I looked up at the rig dangling like a bracelet over the edge of the overpass. Rohn pulled our truck over, and he, my Auntie Annie, and I watched while above us police cars, fire trucks, tow trucks, and paramedics accumulated in the blackness. Out there in the cool black desert, beyond reach of Los Angeles, a man was trapped in the rig's cab, hanging above the road we were taking. Our road was blocked off, so there were a couple of dozen cars both before and behind us. I was surprised there were even that many. These days people didn't drive much for recreational purposes, so the highways were often empty. I climbed out of the truck and wrote on a piece of paper, "The man is going to fall and die." And then I burned the paper. I was superstitious and thought I could prevent bad things from happening by writing them down and burning the paper.

Rohn leaned over my aunt and out the passenger window. "Francie, we don't mind if you believe in that stuff, but you put out that fire good." I stomped on the ashes, stood up to watch the rig. In a moment Rohn leaned out again. "Maybe you shouldn't stand on those ashes. It might be bad luck." I laughed. When I'd first moved in with my aunt and Rohn five years earlier, he hadn't believed in any of my superstitions, but now he'd developed some of his own.

He wrapped his arm around Auntie, and I waited outside to give them a romantic moment alone. The way it was today, with people dying or getting arrested or all the time leaving each other, you hated to love people, you really did. But I had to admit I enjoyed watching my aunt and her boyfriend together.

The crowd oohed as the firemen pulled the truck driver from the cab, and we down below applauded, our claps ringing out sharply into the emptiness. Then the firemen and the driver— who I saw now was actually a woman—waved to us, hugely and theatrically, and one person even bowed, as if the accident had been a planned entertainment.

"Off we go, wenches!" shouted Rohn, and I hopped in.

Before everything ran out of money, back at the beginning of the century, the government had started to build something in Southern California called the Sunshine System, an ambitious series of highways and freeways that would link the whole area and eliminate traffic jams. They never finished the Sunshine though, and the truncated roads arched over the landscape like half of concrete rainbows. You saw them all over, huge concrete forms throwing shadows over the concrete below them. Now, because we were behind schedule anyway, Auntie Annie, Rohn, and I decided to do something we'd always talked about. We snuck up an abandoned rainbow and leaned over the edge where a road abruptly stopped. We felt as if we'd reached the end of the world.

Below us, a car whizzed by on the interstate. Rohn howled, barked, growled, and scratched and shook his butt. He loved making like an animal. He got quite into it sometimes. We waited for him to quiet down.

Auntie Annie looked at him lovingly. Though she was forty-three, only once before in her life had she had a boyfriend, a man she'd chased hard when she was eighteen, in the twenties. She'd followed him to seven states—living with him in three—and finally had fallen out of love as abruptly as she'd fallen in it. The next time she'd fallen in love was when she met Rohn, almost twenty years after her first affair.

Both Annie and Rohn were huge, corpulent, and surprisingly light on their feet. Either Annie's eyebrows had fallen out or she shaved them. Every morning before Rohn or I woke up, she drew long sloping black brows above her eyes, and she drew another long sloping black line on her eyelids, making their slant even more pronounced. She had jet-black hair that she wore to her shoulders—Rohn wore his dark hair to his waist.

"Hey! Look at this. A hair donut," said Rohn now. He lifted his shirt to expose his hairy stomach and squished the flesh around his belly button so that the belly button looked like the hole of a donut.

"Oh, now stop that!" said Auntie.

I laughed as he continued. I could see he was on a roll. "Do Igor!" I said. He leaned over, dragging his foot along the edge of the highway as a glob of saliva fell from his mouth. I was eighteen, another generation from my aunt. Girls of my generation were hard to make sick. I dragged my foot along behind me and let drool fall onto my blouse. Auntie was the only person we acted this way around. It drove her mad.

"I can't look," she said, turning away. She immediately turned back with an annoyed expression. But Rohn grabbed and hugged her, and she smiled reluctantly, wiping saliva from his face with a lace handkerchief. I limped down the road a bit and sat with my legs hanging through a railing. Auntie and Rohn ignored me a lot, treating me at times with a sort of distracted warmth. But I knew that Rohn and I had her wrapped around our fingers. She was kind, a sucker, really. Annie had taken care of me since my parents died of lung cancer in the same year, when I was thirteen. They'd probably both been exposed to a chemical or something awful that caused their sickness. But I was lucky. A lot of kids these days were on their own by the time they turned sixteen or seventeen. I'd always made myself useful, riding my bicycle to help Annie and Rohn out in their delivery business. I still rode the same bicycle as when I started working for them as a child.

As a child, I'd had vivid dreams, and still did, sometimes. When I was younger, I'd heard things and seen things and felt quite haunted. I heard FBI agents knocking at our door and heard music in my ears, and I saw heads floating in the air. I saw not only my parents but also my Uncle Robin die even before they got sick, and at school I always knew who'd picked me when we played Seven-Up. Some of the other kids were the same way. Later, I read in *Popular Psychology* that such children weren't psychic, they just noticed without realizing it infinitesimal changes in people's expressions, voices, or carriages. It was a survival skill they'd developed. Sometimes I was hopelessly ignorant, but other times I *knew* things. For instance, I knew when Annie and Rohn looked at each other with eyes full of devotion and swore they would always be together that this was not true. I don't know how I knew. Certainly they seemed to be in love. Maybe something outside would separate them. I wasn't sure.

"Okay, enough time wasted!" shouted Rohn. We walked down the road and back toward the highway where we'd parked our car. We were on the way to make a delivery of cigarettes, food, black-market Japanese electronics, and clothes out in the desert. Not many people lived in the desert—water was so hard to get—but there were a few. They loved it, I guess, the loneliness and everything. I always came along for long rides when I could, to relieve my boredom. All my deliveries followed the same route—downtown Los Angeles to richtown. Richtown was what everybody who didn't live there called the Beverly Hills and Brentwood area. Every city had a richtown. Six days a week, I rode up and down Wilshire Boulevard, carrying mostly letters and small packages.

When we reached our truck alongside the highway, two highway patrolmen were shining flashlights into the glove compartment.

"Where've you been? Got a problem?" said one of them. "Was that you guys up there?"

"We were just curious," said my aunt.

They shined bright lights on us and didn't say or do anything. I squinted. Rohn reached for his wallet. I knew it pained him to have to give them anything. But we did have the black-market electronics in back. He handed each of them a ten-gallon gas cred, and they took the creds as nonchalantly as Rohn had pretended to be as he handed them over. The men hopped on their bikes and were gone. I'd been on a bike as fast as theirs once and felt as if the air around me was trying to pull the skin off my face.

The truck was open and a gun missing from the glove compartment, but all the boxes seemed to be there. It was our best gun, but we had another, older one. Auntie Annie didn't want me to own a gun till next year, but I always carried a disposable Mace gun.

The hills sloping up from the highway were littered, and—except for the fake plants mixed in with the real—dry and pale. I was always scheming for and lusting after water creds for the plants I kept at home. Every time I saw the parched grasses of the city or countryside, I thought of my plants. I kept a lot of aglaonema, because I'd read they cleared the air even better than most plants. I didn't want to die the way my parents had.

The truck shook every time a car passed. Rohn pushed in our card and we took off. He turned to Auntie. "We gotta see a movie one of these days. We haven't seen a movie in a long time." She raised her arm and indicated the road and he turned to watch where he was steering. Then he turned all the way around and looked at me. "Want to see a movie with us?"

"Rohn!" I yelled, pointing to the road. He turned forward. Rohn always needed to look at who he was talking to, even when he was driving. All of his friends had stories about how they were driving with him once and he almost ran into something because he was looking at them as he talked. The climax of these stories was when the friend took on an expression of mock terror and yelled out, "Rooohn!"

"Watch the road, Rohnny," I said.

He turned all the way around again. "What? I didn't catch that." He laughed and turned back.

The farther you got from the city, the more blank white or outdated billboards you saw. So few people lived in the desert it didn't make much sense to advertise out there. We passed a board for Everest cigarettes, but Everest cigarettes didn't even exist anymore. That's what I loved about the desert. It was on a different schedule than we in the city were on. Sometimes as we drove down the interstate, I tried to imagine that it really was years earlier. They were just starting the Sunshine System, and my parents hadn't been born yet.

As usual, Annie and Rohn were ignoring me as we drove. When I was younger I used to lean out and expose my breasts to truck drivers, so they would honk at us and surprise my aunt and Rohn.

There was something thrilling about the desert, something violent. The desert's rare but violent rainstorms, and especially the ferocious daytime heat, made me feel thrillingly vulnerable. That's what I thought about on that safe, peaceful evening as we drove through the Mojave.

Because we made deliveries at no cost to a motel owner, we always got a room free. The town was nearly empty—a pharmacist/herbalist/chicken farmer; a grocer/palm reader/ mechanic; a motel owner/cook/cowboy/mayor; and maybe a hundred others.

When we got to our room, nothing happened when we switched on the lights. There were brownouts all the time no matter where you lived, so we just unpacked in the darkness and sat on the beds to talk.

"I don't know about that left tire," said Rohn quietly. "I don't know how much longer it'll last." The treads were worn unevenly—something wrong with the struts.

I stood at the open window, saw trucks moving down a highway beyond a long field. It was surreally quiet out. All I could hear was the sound of an endless line of trucks on the highway. Or maybe that low, low rumble was just the wind over the fields.

"There's always my savings," said Annie. She kept half her savings with her, and the other half stashed in secret places. A light began to blink in the room. It was the clock blinking off and on to alert us that we should reset it and the brownout was over. "We'll get new struts tomorrow."

Everything was too serious. It seemed like a good time to go snort-wild. I mumbled, "Honk, honk," and snorted softly. Auntie gave me a now-don't-you-start look. I raised my eyebrows at Rohn and he mumbled, "Honk, honk." I started yelling, "Honk," and snorting until my nostrils were killing me.

"You are an animal!" Rohn shouted gleefully. "An animal!" He began to sing his favorite song. He was way off key but Annie loved his singing and hopped up to dance with him. Despite their light feet, the floor shook. I left them alone for a while, as I did every night when we were away from home like this.

There was a light on in the pharmacy so I went down to buy an herb drink. The guy who owned the pharmacy used to live in richtown but had come here to retire after he'd lost much of his money. Hardly anybody was as rich as they'd once been, and if they were, they probably wouldn't be for long. Today a lot of things you needed for everyday life could be made by people you knew. If you bought from them, you could avoid the twelve and a half percent sales tax. For instance, I never bought packaged shampoo anymore. I bought shampoo from a lady down the street from our home in Hollywood. Every time I had none left, I just brought her my empty bottle and she filled it up.

Nobody was in the herb store, but I let myself in. All the herb jars had prices on them. I set some money down, got a cup, and drank gotu kola until my head spun; and then I went back out.

In the field, under the stars faded by pollution even this far from the city, I felt trust. I trusted the desert. It didn't lie to you. The shapes of the cholla cacti and Joshua trees were clear and harsh against the sky. I sat on a rock. A lot of people over the years had sat on the rocks out there. In the dirt lay cans so rusted you couldn't tell what they'd once held, and shards of glistening glass with edges as smooth as Rohn's voice when he was conning someone. I watched the endless trail of trucks, an enormous lighted power plant towering beyond them in the town across the highway and field.

"Tie up my hands!"

I jumped up and pulled out my Mace gun, but it was only Max the Magician. He was a beggar who lived out there and performed marvelous magic tricks for money. My aunt didn't like him, but I thought he was harmless. Max threw a rope at me and held out his hands. I tied him up as best I could. Since I'd never been in the Child Corps or anything, I didn't know much about knots, but I still think I tied him firmly. He spun around once and when he spun back toward me his hands were untied.

"You can do better than that," he said. His light eyes were always sly and wary. I tied him up again. This time he stayed turned around for a fraction of a second before he spun back. "That was better." He pulled a paper daisy from behind my head and waited expectantly after he'd placed it in my lap.

Having just paid for the gotu kola, all I had left were a few coins and some water credits. There'd been rationing for as long as I could remember. The government sent you gas and drinking-water creds every month and debited your bank account for them. I handed him the coins and he thanked me heartily. He sat on another rock and we listened to the sound of trucks rumbling.

"Where do you think they're always going?" I said.

He looked at me slyly, but it might have meant anything. Those trucks scared me. I felt as if everything in the world was falling apart and yet the trucks kept driving. Every time we came out to the desert, there they were.

"I noticed you had some water creds in there."

I thought I'd hidden them from him. I felt the weight of my Mace in my pocket. I clutched the Mace and shrugged to Max.

"Would you like some water?" he said.

"What do you mean? Do you have any?"

"I might." He pulled a deck of cards out and held it toward me. I chose one. "Jack of clubs," he said.

I stuck the card back in the deck. "You know you're right."

"Is your family on the market for some water?"

"Everybody's on the market." I wondered what lay behind his sly eyes.

"Not everybody can afford it."

"I'll ask them," I said casually. "We might have some money."

"Maybe I'll talk to them tomorrow." His hands were folded primly in his lap, and I stared at one of them. The moonlight and light from the power plant caught a small black bump under his skin. He saw me looking and smiled sadly, then leaned over and bit the bump. "Ptooey," he said, dramatically, and spit something into his hand. The bump was bleeding now and he was holding a shiny black object. It looked like a pearl, lovely, black, shining. This was not one of his magic tricks. It was some sort of skin disease. Both my parents had had it. Those little pearls—so pretty, so grotesque. Max was staring at the ground, seeming almost ashamed.

I still didn't know whether that was the sound of the wind or of the trucks. The wind blew against my ears. It was strange to see shame in a face that usually showed little emotion. I started to tell him about my parents, but he jumped up and commanded me to close my eyes. I obeyed, knowing that when I opened them he would be gone. A scratch. A rustle. Another scratch. I opened my eyes to an empty field. Behind me, the light was still off at the motel. I stretched out my legs in front of me and admired the muscles from all the riding I did. Ever since mail delivery had been privatized, business had been thriving. Some deliverers were on God's time—an hour to them was a month to everybody else. The summer my parents first got sick, I'd been working in Chicago in an umbrella factory and living with a friend's family. I'd sent my parents a package, a beautiful stained-glass mobile an older friend of mine had made. I thought Mom and Dad could hang it up in their hospital room. I was back out in California when they died, and the mobile still hadn't arrived. A year later, the delivery service returned it to me, saying the addressee had moved and left my home as a forwarding address.

White clouds like ribs hung in the sky near the moon. I jumped at a noise, but it was just two lizards scampering over the dirt. I liked lizards. I thought they had tender hearts. I used to own two lizards for pets and one of them, the smaller one, always slept on top of the larger, even though there was a lot of space and he could have slept anywhere. I looked back toward the motel. The lights were still off. Maybe there was another brownout, though usually they occurred in the afternoon or early evening. Maybe Auntie and Rohn were in there having great gushy sex. He adored her as much as she adored him, but what he adored wasn't her so much as the way that she adored him. Well, maybe he also adored her skin. She made everybody touch it at least once. She had the softest skin in the world. It was her glory.

Auntie Annie and my father had been close, at least as close as people got these days. Besides Auntie, I had not got truly close to anyone, even Rohn. There was no percentage in it. For all I knew, everyone I knew was dying. When my parents had died, Annie wanted to bury them in one of those expensive cemeteries like where Uncle Robin was. The grounds were always well guarded, but I didn't like the thought of my parents lying there while security guards with rifles marched around. I wanted my parents to be at peace. So we'd cremated them and had them buried in vases in a cremation burial ground. Even that had been robbed, the vases stolen. I thought the earth where dead people lay was different from other earth in some spiritual and not at all imaginary way, and I couldn't believe that graves were dug up as frequently as they were.

I always carried a pouch containing a couple of rocks from a rock garden my parents had made for me once. Now I reached into my pocket—the one opposite my gun—and took out my rocks. In my mind, Mom was the round one, and Dad, the triangular one. When I was feeling severely troubled, I took out my parents and talked to them as if they were still alive, but for now I put them back in their pouch.

"Hey, Francie!" Rohn was bellowing. "Fancy-Francie!" I jumped up and turned around. "We're going to feast."

I ran as fast as I could back toward the motel, realizing as I ran how hungry I was. When I caught up with Rohn and Auntie, we walked quickly toward the diner.

"I was talking to Max, and he said he might have some water we can buy."

"Guaranteed clean?" said my aunt.

"I guess so. He didn't say. . . . I have forty water creds but I don't have any money with me."

"I told you not to talk to Max," my aunt said, as if suddenly remembering she didn't like him.

"He's okay. I feel bad for him. He has derma-what-do-you-call-it. I saw the thing in his hand."

Annie raised her own hand and looked at it. I recoiled, but her skin was clear. The disease wasn't fatal or really even harmful, but there was something profoundly disturbing about it.

"I'll talk to him tomorrow," Rohn said.

The café was empty now, except for the cook and a couple of his kids. He had a daughter around my age, but she was a chirp. Everything was fine and wonderful and terrif with her. There was a riot every day in one city or another, but everything was fine. When I went to school a few years earlier, we used to play practical jokes on the chirps. It was mean-spirited of us, but I thought they were mean in their own way too.

Annie had her arm around Rohn and she was leaning into him on their side of our booth. She looked as happy as she always did when he was around.

When the cook came to our table, Rohn asked about Max's water.

The cook lowered his voice. "He's really got some, I heard. I don't know where he got it."

"Did you buy any?" I said.

"No, I wouldn't touch his water. That guy makes me nervous. You never know if he's behind you or where. You can't be too careful."

Just about everybody broke laws all the time—the Consumption Law, the black-market laws, the licensing laws. There was probably nobody in the entire country, except a few chirps, who couldn't be arrested for *something*. Occasionally, the police arrested a randomly chosen person, and if you went searching for him or her, they might arrest you, too.

We ate like pigs, gorging ourselves on tacos. There was nothing fresh in our dinners at all. Everything canned or synthetic. I can't honestly say the bad food dampened our appetites. We scorched the table in a celebration of bad food.

Later, back in my room, I couldn't sleep, and then when I did sleep I had vivid dreams about all of us. I also dreamed my rocks had escaped, so when I woke in the middle of the night I took them into the bathroom to talk to them. Outside, I could hear the sound of trucks, or wind, and when I peeked out I saw the line of trucks, moving at a steady speed.

The bathroom floor was the nicest thing about our room. The floor was high-grade foamite, very soft and warm. I took out my parents and asked them if they still loved each other. I made them have satisfying rock sex together, and then I put them away and went back to bed.

Max came over early, even before Rohn had a chance to deliver any packages, and we went to look at the water. Max kept the water in a ghost ghost-town. About fifty years in the past, the town had been a tourist attraction, but these days, many tourist attractions had gone under. The ghost ghost-town was just a few wooden buildings with a main street. Inside a shack called Town Hall, Max poured us a couple of ounces each of water. It tasted sweet and pure.

"How much do you have?" I said, feeling desire rising in me.

"Enough for all your needs."

"What are you charging?" said my aunt.

"Five dollars cash and five gas creds for each gallon."

"That's ridiculous." She sneezed daintily. She did everything daintily despite her size. But she was a good bargainer. "Two dollars cash and two gas credits for each one."

"Four and two."

"One and three."

"Three and two."

"Sold." She started to count out her savings.

"Aw, wait," said Rohn. "I'll pay half. Francie needs the water."

"Don't you want to see the water first?" said Max, looking at Rohn.

"All right, let's go." Annie handed Rohn her money and the two men walked away.

"You guys wait in the truck," said Max as they were leaving.

Back in the truck, I stared out at the desert. It seemed at once monotonous and full of nuance. I could think that I was seeing nothing at all but dirt, and suddenly the "dirt" would move as an animal changed position. After about fifteen minutes, Auntie and I looked at each other at the same time, saying nothing. "I'll go find him," I finally said.

The building we'd been in was empty, except for a bottle of water. I picked it up and put on the cap and went to search for Rohn and Max. But they were nowhere. I searched in each of the small buildings, then returned to the first. On a table, right in the middle, lay our money. I didn't know whether I hadn't noticed it before, or whether someone had put it there within the past few minutes. But I knew what it meant. It was a warning, to tell me that Rohn had been arrested, not robbed. I put the money in my pocket, and, clutching the water, hurried back to the truck.

"Hurry, we have to go," I said. "He's been arrested." I stuffed the money in her pocketbook. "Maybe they'll come for us." I stunned even myself by how cold-hearted I was, by how my only thought now was of Annie and me. But it wouldn't do any good for all three of us to get arrested. "Be calm," I said, even though Annie was perfectly calm.

She drove grimly back to the motel. We hurried to our room, as if that would protect us somehow. After a few minutes, Annie said, "I have to get you out of here," though I'd just been thinking I had to get *her* out. There was much that Rohn—and all of us—could have been arrested for. But I suppose that whoever had arrested Rohn had figured he was the head of the delivery business. In fact, Auntie was half owner.

It seemed to me that the trip back to Los Angeles was unnaturally short, not unnaturally long as I would have expected. When we reached our home, I felt dazed. In the distance a couple of different sirens were going off. I could hear a mechanical voice: "You are trespassing on private property. The police will arrive soon." Another mechanical voice spoke in a

loud monotone: "Help me. Help me." Someone must have
walked by still another alarm, because I heard a mechanical
burp as the person passed but didn't stop.

I lay in bed with my eyes opened, and when morning came,
I went about my routine. I was nothing if not adaptable. That
was me, Queen of the Adapts. I felt that morning as if many
people and things—from my parents to Rohn to the constant
noise of alarms and traffic—were like that music I used to hear,
but I wanted to forget it, wanted it to go away, at least for a
little while. I watered a couple of plants, some giant birds of
paradise, and a canna lily with huge red flowers. I always in-
serted polymers into the soil to make the dirt retain more water.
I knew just how much water to give my plants. Plants and I had
an understanding. I loved them and they needed me. I like how
I could exert control over whether they lived or died.

When I'd gone back inside, something thumped on our glass
back door, and when I looked up, a cat I'd fed once was throwing
itself against the glass. It was weird, the way that skinny thing
kept hitting the door. When I let him in, he rubbed against my
leg. I poured him some water and he drank a full cup, more
water than I'd ever seen a cat drink at once, and he ate a small
can of mixed fish. I always bought myself mixed fish now; tuna
had become too expensive. Afterward, I reached down to pet
him but he hissed and ran outside. I went to sit on the back
porch and watched the cat watching me. The porch was painted
dusty red. Rohn and I had painted it together. The light from
the yellow-tinged sky shone on my smooth skin, and I noticed
a bump on my forearm. I took a safety pin from off my bra and
pricked my skin, watched the small black pearl fall to the ground
and settle in the dirt. The sight of that made me feel tired, too
tired to reach down to pick up the pearl or examine my skin
further. The disease was harmless, like acne, but I felt so tired

I could scarcely move. I lay back and watched butterflies cross paths over me.

I didn't know what Auntie was up to, probably crying. I wondered whether it wasn't time for me to go off on my own, to move away. I'd been planning for a while to move out later that year, and I guessed that was still the plan. I just wished I knew where I could go, *now*. I also had a conflicting feeling, that there ought to be a Home Day, when everybody who'd ever left came back. But the more I thought about it, the more I saw it wouldn't work. How could you tell which of your past homes you belonged at? I thought then that there were two reasons in the world to cry—because you *were* at home, with people you were for better or for worse attached to; or because you weren't at home. But I didn't know.

Over the next week, Auntie Annie started to expand. Already corpulent, she seemed to get obese overnight. It had always been an experience to watch her and Rohn eat with the relish of gluttons, but now she ate with the shame of one. Every day, she put on an old, thin T-shirt of Rohn's, worn inside out. Her pants didn't fit anymore, so she left the zipper open, and she seemed to have given up all hope of ever zipping them. With her pants open, her wrinkled belly was exposed. I'd never seen her belly before. I was surprised by the wrinkles and wondered whether she'd ever been pregnant. It was sad to see her sit on the back porch, watching the branches move with the wind for hours. Once, seeing a bumblebee land near her, I remembered the time Rohn had been stung by a bee on his neck, and later that night Annie's neck had started to hurt, as if she, too, had been stung.

On her birthday, a week and a half after Rohn's disappearance, she sat outside alone. Her face was shiny with gold-speckled sunscreen. She'd got ugly with a speed that shocked me. I kept thinking, "That's not the way she really looks, not the way she looks now." Her skin got dull, and pouches on her face made her eyes seem small, squished for room. But no matter what, she always managed to paint on her sloping black eyebrows.

I let her work in my garden, which was a mess. Neatness was not my interest; growth was. Once, she spent an hour trimming a bush until its wild growth was turned into a few stubs with uneven branches sticking out here and there.

Some days, there was a complete breakdown of pretension. She farted all the time, loud rumbling farts which somehow had the effect of breaking my heart. She screamed and yelled and sang and murmured. She stayed home always.

Like her, I never felt like making any deliveries, and every day I made fewer. I didn't know how we were going to pay our property and living taxes. I wanted to drive away, away from the sirens and alarms of the city. One day, I didn't make any deliveries at all. My muscles were already losing their tone. My plants were fading fast. When I looked at the sky, and saw how yellow the blue was, I didn't feel like doing anything except reading maps and thinking of where I could go. I had black pearls growing between my toes.

The next morning, Auntie Annie knocked on my door and said "Hi!" like a chirp or something.

"What's with you?" I said.

"I don't know. I thought it was a nice day," she said. Chirp. Chirp. For a second her sadness passed like an eclipse over her face. But then she rallied. "It's nice out!" she said again. Chirp! I couldn't tell what her problem was, but finally she announced, "I'm going back to try to find Rohn. You wait here." She spoke as if she'd just said she was going to the store for cottage cheese.

I sat in my room, listening to the truck start. She just up

and left, without packing. I thought about Rohn disappearing, about how now Auntie would possibly disappear, too.

"Annie!" I yelled, but she was gone. I decided to chase her on my bicycle. I knew which route she would take, and by weaving in the heavy traffic, I was sure I'd be able to catch her. As I rode, the four things I always carried bounced around in my pockets—the pouch with my parents, my Mace gun, my wallet with water creds, and a twig from a plant Auntie and Rohn had given me once. My mind kept telling me to turn back, but my legs wouldn't listen.

A Cage of Light

Then it was the opposite: my tired legs told me to turn back, but my mind refused to consider it. I never caught up, riding long after there was any hope of catching her. When I finally returned home, I sat alone on the back porch, the official thinking place in our home. My legs were unused to riding and already felt sore. I tried to decide what to do next. I was responsible for myself as never before. A part of me felt excited by that, if only the circumstances could have been different. Fatigue made me calm. I would call Auntie at the motel later that night.

Meanwhile, my plants were drying out. I got up to

water them. Sometimes, as now, it seemed like too much pressure to be responsible for them. I wanted to rip them out by
their roots and be done with them. I watered and fed them
instead. When I was finished, I went inside and turned on the
floor heater just because the musty familiar smell comforted me.
I enjoyed the feeling of the heat making my loose shorts billow
around my yellow-brown legs—the yellow from my Japanese
mother, the brown from my Chinese-black father.

Toward the end, my parents were bitter about their im-
pending deaths, but it was a bitterness broken up by bursts of
almost searingly intense sincerity, bursts during which they tried
to teach me everything they knew and to instill in me the desire
to know even more. Their lessons didn't take. I cared for my
plants and my bicycle, but not for knowledge. I believed it was
not my knowledge but my skill and my strength that would help
me conquer the future, the present, and even the past. They
didn't know I felt this. During those last days, they even asked
me to take notes on what they were saying. I was what they
possessed on those early mornings when they might have woken
from a dream to face the dark, unclear outlines of their hospital
beds. I was the answer to their questions, questions about their
lives and about their deaths—to the extent that the two could
now be separated. The sky on those early mornings would still
have been gray, and through the locked hospital windows they
might have heard the sound of an occasional ambulance or a
car, or maybe, if they were lucky, a bird or two.

The first time I saw the bitterness of my mother was during
a respite from the hospital. As we were taking a walk, I com-
mented on the lights of the city and she bent over a mound of
dirt and picked up a handful. "Put out your palm," she demanded. I put it out and she dropped the dirt into it. "That's
how much light weighs. Don't let it fool you." She quoted from
an ancient poem, about how we all live in a cage of light. I felt

betrayed by her bitterness and her sickness. I remember thinking that I'd like to throw the dirt at her as she started to walk away. For a moment, I stood indecisively, hating her and loving her, then dropped the dirt and ran to catch up.

That same day, I had been waiting with my father in the reception room of a medical clinic. He'd made an appointment, but we still had to wait several hours. When a doctor peeked into the room, my father got so mad he threatened to rip the faces off every doctor in the place and mop up the blood with their hair. He spoke passionately, as if he were shouting about liberating the earth, particularly that small portion of the earth in the waiting room. The other patients, some of whom had waited even longer than us, looked up heavy-lidded, bored, and then looked down to their magazines after the doctor agreed to see my father. That was my parents in the end. During those last few weeks, I saw them as majestic and cruel, harsh and affectionate, the product of every kiss, and every slight, that had ever touched their radiance. They were radiant to me in a way that Auntie Annie and Rohn had never been. But now, as the floor heater began to burn my legs, I looked around at the cluttered house I'd lived in for five years, and I realized I'd underestimated Auntie and Rohn.

But I felt suddenly overcome by a need for busywork. I turned off the heater and examined my plants, tending to them in a way I hadn't done for a couple of weeks. Colonies of aphids had attacked my hibiscus, and my lemon tree seemed to be suffering from iron deficiency. The aglaonema were too hardy to have been affected by my inattention. Every thirty minutes, I called the motel, and finally, several hours later, my aunt picked up.

"Hello?" There seemed to be several question marks behind that tentative "hello."

"Annie, it's me. I can't believe you just went off that way.

It's dangerous. You need to be careful. What are you doing? What do you *think* you're doing? What *are* you doing? You have to watch out for yourself. Do you have a plan? Anything could happen to you out there." I hadn't meant to have a rant, but couldn't stop myself. Sometimes, as when I was talking about something important, or kissing a boy I really liked, or eating fresh food, my mouth went out of control. Now I paused for breath.

Auntie Annie jumped in. "I *am* watching out for myself. That's what I'm doing out here."

"When are you coming back?"

I heard her making throat noises, a quirk that showed up sometimes when she was thinking. "When I find him."

"He might not even be where you can find him."

There were a couple of gurgly noises and a sort of burp. "I guess I'll be home next week."

"If you're not, I'm going out there."

"Don't you want to hear what I've found out?"

"What? Have you talked to anyone?"

"Everyone at the café says they haven't seen Max around at all. Of course that's not too unusual, but it is a little odd. Anyway, don't come after me. Maybe I'll be back sooner."

"I'll call you tomorrow," we said at the same time, and then we hung up.

It was getting late. Rather than shower I rubbed myself reasonably clean with a dry towel, washed my hands, and got in bed. There was a creak in the wall near the closet, as well as creaking from outside. I listened to wall spirits crying, floor spirits crying, wind spirits, sky spirits, heart spirits. I fell asleep. I woke and fell asleep repeatedly. I felt both fitful and strong that night, fitful because I feared losing both Rohn and my aunt, but strong because I knew I had to be. I felt strangely enthralled with the brutality of the world I had to face.

Two mornings later, Annie was back, asleep in her room, and I felt relieved that I wouldn't have an opportunity to test myself—yet. I went out to work in the front yard before getting ready to make some deliveries. In our front yard a giant bird of paradise plant reached almost as high as the star of the yard—our thirty-foot-tall jacaranda tree. The bird of paradise—a smaller variety, not what we grew—was the official flower of Los Angeles. The one in our yard possessed leaves as tall as ten and a half feet—exactly twice as tall as me—and pointy slate-blue flowers that grew improbably out of the gut of the plant and looked like the heads of primordial birds. I did not find these plants paradisical, but to me they would have made a more fitting choice for an official flower than the smaller, prettier variety, because they looked the way I saw Los Angeles—surprising and violent, full of hidden savage beauties.

When Auntie woke up, she was neither the chirp-like creature of yesterday nor the burping, murmuring glutton of the week before. For the first time ever, I saw her without black lines drawn over her eyes. She had the face of a girlish boy, with eyes that were soft but showed signs of future hardness. She had long straight lashes, and the corners of her eyes curved slightly at the end of their slant. When I left to make my deliveries, she was writing letters to help her find Rohn, and when I returned several hours later, she was still writing letters. Besides his friends, I wasn't sure whom she might be writing to. I thought she might even be using a phone book, writing to everyone in the book in order. Earlier, when I'd asked her what had happened, she said she'd searched the ghost ghost-town, and asked questions of everyone she'd met. No one knew anything, and Max the Magician never showed up. She didn't know what to do next. Having lost my parents, I could understand her hurt, but I couldn't understand the way she refused to accept that Rohn was gone.

"But don't you love him?" she asked.

"Sure, I did, but he's gone," I said. She seemed worried when I said that. She wasn't worried because Rohn was gone but because of my coldness. But I didn't want to spend time worrying about her worry. I had even more work than usual to do while she was incapacitated by Rohn's absence. All I did was ride my bicycle and take care of my plants.

After a few weeks, the delivery business started to flag. Annie had lost interest in anything but her letters, and we lived partly on savings. I got a job as a waitress at a place called House of Burgers. Most of the dinners on the menu were composed of cheap or even fake meat, but we did have one good beef meal for people who wanted to splurge. My weeks at House of Burgers were boring, yet they passed quickly. I had my first affair with a grownup, sort of, a former member of the Frog Club children's television show. He worked as a cook now. Whenever we had sex, he liked me to yell "Take me! Take me!" at certain crucial moments, and I wondered whether this was what adult sex was all about. He had played a character called Peter Polywog. Once, as we stood at an intersection waiting to cross, a carload of boys about my age stuck their heads out the windows and started yelling, "Hey, it's Peter Polywog!" They were genuinely excited, but he was humiliated. Sometimes I asked him to sing me a song from his TV days, but he refused, unless he was drunk. Then he would burst into song: "The Polywogs Take Over," "Spacefrog," "When Boy Meets Girl." He was funny, but he didn't make my mouth go out of control.

I wasn't a very good waitress. The restaurant manager didn't like me because the cook always brought me flowers (usually fake ones) while I was out on the floor taking orders, and because I couldn't balance the trays of food over my head like the manager wanted. I was always sending bits of pink tofu-ham sprinkling to the floor. One day, when the manager was in a particularly bad mood, my plastic waitress cap fell into the milk-shake mix, and we needed to drain the whole machine. Thus ended my adventure: I was fired from House of Burgers. My Frog Club friend abandoned me for someone more coordinated, a waitress who could carry one tray on her head and one in each hand.

Getting fired depressed me quite a bit. I didn't think I could ever get a job again. Who would hire me? Of course, I knew the job had been just a temporary stop on the way to . . . somewhere. And even in my depression, Los Angeles could seem beautiful and romantic to me, with the way at certain times of day the clouds and mountains glowed like faded neon, and the way the twirling freeways circled the city like a carousel. I saw promise lying alongside disease and decay on every street I passed. Around every corner, I imagined a boy I might fall in love with, despite myself. And there was a whole world to learn about. But still, because of Rohn, a part of my heart was emptied.

Auntie Annie and I lived in a run-down wooden bungalow in Hollywood. Her great-grandmother had bought the house in 1970, when she first got married. I used to sit on the splintery red back porch and dream about cleaning up our jungle of a back yard and throwing a party the way I imagined those girls in richtown with pleated skirts and college futures did. But I didn't like pleated skirts, and I hadn't even graduated from high school.

My aunt, more tough-minded than I'd realized, had begun to make the delivery business work again and had hired new riders to take my place. I could have gone back to work for her, but I didn't want to. I needed something new. It was after an accident that summer—when I'd just turned nineteen—that I decided to go to college. I was walking on the sidewalk when a ninety-year-old man in a car jumped the curb and pinned me momentarily to a wall. As I lay on the sidewalk immediately after, watching his face leaning over mine to see if I was okay, I remember wondering stupidly whether he was in law enforcement—it was illegal for people who weren't to drive cars with the kind of acceleration he must have needed to jump over the curb that way. That's what I was thinking as I lay on the sidewalk, surrounded by people. When the paramedics had been cutting off my clothes, I'd offered to sit up to help them out, and I got so insistent, someone had to hold me down. "No, I want to cooperate," I kept saying, fighting the paramedic off. "Let me help you."

My right arm was crushed, but instinctively I never glanced to the right. I was scared the arm would have to be amputated, even though doctors rarely need to perform amputations these days. The paramedic said everything was going to be okay, and I believed him because I had nothing better to do. He poured some iodine on a leg wound; the iodine stung and I turned my head to grimace. The crowd was excited. "Ooooh, it looks like it really hurts," someone said. I felt oddly satisfied with my grimace, felt it had been dramatic and effective. A tube and bottle were attached to my left arm, I hurt all over, I was numb, scared, and disoriented, and I possessed a vague feeling that I ought to flirt—or at least trade jokes—with the paramedics.

I asked for a painkiller, which they said they weren't allowed to give me since it might interfere with whatever the doctors eventually said I needed. Otherwise, I pretended to be fine, not to seem brave, but because pain is very personal. I wanted everyone to know it hurt because I felt on-stage and show-offy, but I knew no one really understood and I was glad of that.

The car—the cause of it all—was light blue. When it hit as I walked on the sidewalk, I was confused because I wasn't sure what was happening, though I knew it was something terrible. I felt sick and panicky because the situation had no continuity with my former life.

When my aunt arrived, she began apologizing profusely, as was her nature, but at the same time she bossed everybody around. "I'm so sorry to be a bother," she said to the paramedics, "but you'd better take good care of her or I'll have to sue you." The man who hit me was crying, and she told him, "I'm sorry my niece has upset you, but get out of my sight."

Since I didn't have health insurance—few people did—a doctor looked me over and then I waited while Auntie went home to get extra money, so she could pay for the surgery in advance. Auntie cursed the bureaucracy at the same time that she apologized for my not having insurance. She was sorry to be asking so many questions. She was sorry to be getting in the way. She was sorry the doctors were such cold-hearted incompetents. After a while, I'd lost so much blood that no matter how many blankets they laid on me I couldn't stop shivering. I imagined my blood not freezing but drying up. I felt a dry, dry cold, more in my bones than in my flesh. My aunt returned and I heard her screaming to someone, "I'm really sorry that I'm going to have to kill you now." Hours later I got wheeled into the operating room. Right before they put me to sleep, a crazy attendant in a surgical mask furtively took my hand and whispered, "You're my long-lost wife! I'm going to bring you to New Jersey and take care of you!" And then they put me out.

When I woke I was still in California, and the crazy attendant was nowhere to be seen.

I was hospitalized almost five weeks, in a room with a woman who watched TV all day and a girl who watched all night. Mostly they watched the news, twenty-four hours a day of riots and shortages, of the dissolution of the only world I'd ever known. Breathing the stale air of the hospital, sealed off from the noises and smells and risks of life, I felt safe, in a way I had not felt in a long time. But I hated it. I wanted out. The woman who watched TV all day was a malingerer—she played tricks on the doctors to make them think she was sicker than she was. Sometimes she sat on hot-water bottles, sometimes on ice, to try to alter her temperature, and she took pills that made her throw up. She did all this secretly, or tried to, but sometimes the other girl and I saw her. By some agreement of looks and glances and raised eyebrows, nobody spoke about the woman's secret. Let her stay in the hospital if she wanted. Some people might think she was taking up a hospital bed that would be better given over to someone who was physically sick, but to me, if she needed to go to all the trouble she went to, then she was entitled. She needed help, but what help would there be for her if she was released?

After days of boredom, I started to do something I hadn't done since I was a child: I prayed. Toward the end of my stay, I sometimes prayed for a few hours a day. I prayed for Rohn, Auntie Annie, my parents, my hospital roommates, and everyone I'd ever known that I could think of. I had a lot of time. I didn't pray to God but rather to the small patch of sky I could see from our window.

When I got out of the hospital, I told my aunt that I'd decided to go to college. "Why?" she asked me.

I wasn't sure. Maybe it had something to do with knowledge and with my parents, or maybe it was because whenever things weren't going well for me, I became contradictorily hopeful. I became focused on whatever small patches of sky I could see. And school had come to seem like one of those patches.

Auntie Annie burst into tears, and mumbled something about Rohn and about school, and then she ran to her room. Rohn would have been delighted by my decision, but then he was often delighted about something. He was just a delighted person, as Auntie Annie had been when he was around.

The bungalow we lived in was getting more run down every month. The most beautiful thing about our house—about the whole neighborhood, really—was the purple-flowered jacaranda tree in our front yard, a few feet in front of our giant bird of paradise. The tree had been planted around the turn of the century. It was so radiant—and on such a defeated, ugly street—that on a number of occasions strangers knocked on our front door to express admiration. Sometimes Rohn invited these people in. He was the friendliest, most talkative person I ever met. He even talked to birds and dogs. He sincerely liked those animals, but at the same time he was something of a con man so he was always practicing his charm on them. Once, I peeked out the back porch and saw a crow sitting on his knee, and dogs were all the time hanging around our front door. One animal we all hated was rats, Rohn and Auntie because rats were scavengers and carried diseases; and I, because they were surely bad luck.

Auntie had her garrulous moments but was more prone to meditation than Rohn was. Though she was no chirp, she favored chirpy items like HOME, SWEET HOME signs, stuffed animals, and anything with flowers printed on it. We kept Christmas ornaments on display year round, because they pleased her, and for as long as I could remember we'd owned a welcome mat that said "Enter with a Smile" on it. Even our house alarm said, "Please don't make me alert the police."

Auntie saved dozens of old plastic bottles that she filled unlabeled with household liquids, so that you might think you were about to pour on some fragrant shampoo and instead found yourself with a headful of floorglo. Besides being a saver, Auntie was kind-hearted, often excessively so. For instance, she'd read that when plants are dying they emit a high-pitched noise, so she became very upset when one of my plants died, because she thought the poor thing was crying, only we couldn't hear it. And then she didn't like to throw it out, because she thought it might only be hibernating. I have to admit there were moments when I thought so, also. Come to think of it, I was the one who gave her the idea. So I didn't really mind anything about our home. I was becoming sort of a barbarian, myself. At home I liked to eat with my fingers, use my shirt sleeve to wipe my mouth, and put my feet on the dining room table, even when others were eating. I made odd noises when I ate, but Auntie and Rohn never minded because they made louder noises and probably couldn't hear me.

Many nights, my aunt and Rohn had fox-trotted or waltzed in the living room. The dancing made me secretly optimistic about the world, because I knew they'd both been unhappy previously, for most of their lives, in fact—deceived by friends, neighbors, lovers, or co-workers, deceived by their own hopes, goals, and abilities. And then they became happy. So I believed anything was possible. Everything always worked out. And that was how I met the world that autumn.

Hope

We lived in a section of town largely abandoned by anyone who mattered to the country's economy. Statistically, nonwhites and poor whites made up sixty-four percent of the population but made only twenty percent of the legal purchases. But the county government, which tended to be progressive in its policies, helped to fund a two-year college in my area that didn't require a high school degree. All you needed was to be older than eighteen and able to pass a basic reading test that eliminated half the adult population of Hollywood. I started at the college in September.

I worked for the school paper, where most of the

students were in their thirties or late twenties, and many were older. Several had drinking or emotional problems that prevented them from holding full-time jobs, and almost all of them possessed a cunning that I both envied and feared, and eventually realized that I, too, possessed. The cunning was a sword against the world, the way wealth was a shield for the people of richtown. What lay underneath all the cunning was hope. I learned later, when I met some students who'd attended universities, that what mostly separated us from the students at universities was they held expectations of the world, whereas what we had was hope. That never changed for me. Sometimes I longed to have that ease, to be a person who expected, but I couldn't. I felt I didn't have rights so much as hopes. But in the end I always found hope was enough.

Not everybody possessed even hope. There was a nominal tuition, plus extensive work-study programs, and several people had been in the two-year journalism program for as long as ten years. I could see how it would be hard to leave, unsure as we all were about what we were in school for in the first place. And yet I would have to leave eventually, because that was the whole point.

I first walked into the campus city room in the middle of my second semester. It was sort of a whim—I didn't have a major yet. The city room was about twenty by twenty feet, including two offices—each with two desks—set off by flimsy partitions. To the side was a normal office for the department head. That is, it was a tiny room with a real wooden door, and through that was the darkroom, glowing from the safelight and smelling of chemicals. Crammed into the city room were a number of dented metal desks, with old-fashioned word processors screwed into their tops, and there were a couple of shadeless windows and one of those clocks that seemed to be in every classroom from first grade on. Though it was three p.m., the clock's hands pointed to eight. There was a scraping sound in the room, but I didn't know where it came from.

When I'd entered, a woman lifted her head and looked at me steadily for a few seconds. Then she yawned loudly and turned to a magazine she'd been reading. She resembled a worn, toughened version of those blond, heavy-lashed dolls children have, except the doll had been dragged around and broken and fixed again. Her blouse was buttoned wrong, and her nose was crooked. She was kind of great looking, actually. Her voice when she spoke was mostly clear and smooth, but with occasional cracks in it. "Look at this," she said. She pointed to the magazine. Inside was a picture of a man, apparently an actor, with the greenest eyes ever, a strange almost bluish green. "Can you believe that man exists on the same planet I do?" Questions like that always stumped me; I was too literal-minded. When people told jokes, I never got the punchline because I was too busy thinking, But how did this rabbit learn to talk? Or, Why can't something as powerful as a genie manage to get out of a bottle? I mean, where else would the man exist if not on the same planet?

The woman turned to the room, in which a few people were milling about or working at their desks. "This girl can't talk," she announced. She studied the magazine, pushing and tugging at her nose in a way that made my stomach queasy. "She can't talk," she repeated, as a challenge. She made me nervous, so I yawned in her face.

"Don't mind her," said a man. I saw a by-line on his screen—his name was Mark Trang. He had glowing deep-beige skin, and dark-framed glasses rested above his sharp cheekbones. His body was compact, and he had lean, veiny hands. He frowned, then asked whether I'd cut myself shaving—I wore a bandage on my chin. He was teasing, but he also seemed gentle.

"Um," I said. He waited. "I tripped on my front porch."

Mark and another man caught each other's eye. They smiled benignly, almost approvingly, as if they loved all human beings but especially loved human beings who tripped on their front porches and cut their chins. Mark gave four quick taps with his fingertips on his desk; later I learned that whenever he tapped, it signaled a mood change or a sudden thought. I think it was a good gesture for him, because it made you look at his hands. He turned to his desk and began riffling through a file.

The campus paper was a weekly, and that night, Wednesday, was the night the staff completed work on the current issue. Deadline was Thursday morning. I stayed all night at the office, helping write headlines and fillers. A lot of people stayed overnight. In fact, there were almost as many people around at midnight as there had been at three p.m. I felt kind of free there because I knew hardly anyone would read the paper; we could write all sorts of things criticizing anyone we wanted, and none of us would disappear the way Rohn had. The press was as powerful as government, though often as corrupt as well. But I couldn't think of a single instance of a journalist being arrested.

There were ten or fifteen people in the city room: a few writers and editors I didn't talk to; Mark; his best friend, Lucas, a former gang member who wore a necktie that he never loosened all night; Jewel, the woman with the magazine; Joe, twenty-four, who'd never had a girlfriend and kept talking about sex all night; Bernard, who was somewhere in his late thirties and always seemed slightly guilty, as if he were lying to you; and Frank, a photographer with a skin condition. Jewel called him Strudel Face whenever he was out of the room. Jewel was sarcastic, cynical, flippant. I liked her.

Aside from the janitor and one or two campus police, we were the only ones around. I felt that, at least until morning, there were no real obstacles in life except writing the next headline. And it was sort of weird, because sometimes the clock in the city room came to life, jolting forward ten minutes or even an hour at a time. There were no brownouts until ten, and then the lights blinked once and went out. Everyone stopped working and took out something to eat. I hadn't thought to bring anything, but Mark gave me some of what he'd brought—bread that smelled slightly moldy and fresh grapes, a luxury. Mark told me a joke as we sat there in the dark, but I didn't get the punchline. I was too busy thinking, But didn't the bartender think it was unusual when a vampire walked in? Mark smelled faintly of aftershave, faintly of sweat. I could still hear a scraping noise.

"What's that noise?" I said.

"It's the windmills on top of the building."

"But the air's so still out there."

"They're real sensitive. A friend of mine's uncle invented them. I think one is broken, so it makes that noise."

Two men started yelling at each other about which one of them had forgotten to make an important phone call for a story.

"I'm going to get back into yelling," said Mark. "I miss it."

"Don't you ever yell?"

"Not much. Let's see, I think the last time I yelled was two years ago at an ex-girlfriend."

"Why did you yell at her?" I said, as the lights went on.

He blinked at the sudden light, then smiled. "So . . . where do you live?" he said.

I became aware that someone was watching us, and I turned to see Joe across the desk studying Mark and me. He probably just liked to watch men and women talking. I ignored Mark's question and returned to work. Joe got up and left.

For the most part we were all quiet, except for brief outbursts. Once, I was leaning against a wall rubbing my forehead. Frank, who'd just rushed out of the darkroom like a madman, scolded me: "Why are you leaning so hard on that wall?" I laughed, thinking he was kidding. Jewel rolled her eyes. "He's serious," she said. I think she'd rolled her eyes not because she thought he was crazy, but because I hadn't known he was serious. Eventually I found out he always worried about things like chairs and floors and stairs, anything that came under the assault of human pressure. Sometimes when I considered how many truly crazy people there were in the world, I thought it was great; other times I thought it was tragic. Tonight I was too sleepy to care.

After his wall remark, Frank practically attacked Mark, for no apparent reason, and they started wrestling on the floor for a few seconds before Mark could push him away and he returned to the darkroom. Mark said he stayed in there for hours at a time. I pictured him smelling those chemicals in that dull light, consumed with his work, safe from the world and from his own craziness. Jewel grumbled, "Dandruff Face! Strudel Head!"

"Is he a good photographer?" I said. Jewel rolled her eyes again.

"Not really," said Mark.

"Then why put up with him?"

"Because he paid his class fees like everyone else."

When we all finished work, it was still dark and the campus was empty, so the women got walked to their cars. Mark and Lucas came with me. Lucas told me he was twenty-six and had dropped out in the seventh grade. Mark was my age—I'd just turned nineteen. He'd been here for a year and didn't know what to do next. Maybe find a way to transfer to a university. Maybe not. When I asked him where his parents were, he tapped at a chain-link fence. "I'm not sure." I was glad he didn't ask me where mine were. At the car Lucas said good-bye, but Mark didn't say anything, probably still thinking about his parents.

But he smiled when I said good-bye, and I thought there was something buoyant about him.

A few days later, I was studying when Auntie Annie called me into the living room. Mark was standing there, frowning at the shining Christmas ornaments. Annie nodded vigorously at me—she liked him. I could tell she was dying to have a word with me. Whenever she first met boys I knew, she gave me her impressions in one line, and then she never tried to sway my opinion again. She'd say, "His pants are too tight" or "His shirt is too loose" or "His pants are too tight and his shirt is too loose." That meant she hated him. Now she leaned in and whispered to me, "He smells much better than your last boy-friend." That meant she loved him.

Mark and I decided to drive to House of Burgers to eat. When we got there and sat down, the night manager eyed me suspiciously, and the cook, whom I hadn't seen in months, burned our orders—two Wild West Unburgers. I pounded the bottom of the ketchup bottle, and a glop fell on my lap and dripped over the side of my thigh as I watched. When I reached for a napkin, there were none in the dispenser. "I could have sworn there were a bunch of napkins in there," I said.

"Oh, sorry," Mark said. He reached into a bulge in his jacket and pulled out a napkin. "Here."

"Um, thanks."

He studied me frankly. (Later we talked about that night and he said I was studying *him* frankly.) "I have an important question," he finally said.

"What?"

"Why do you have Christmas ornaments hung in your house?"

"They're pretty."

"I didn't say they weren't pretty. They *look* fine."

"No, I mean that's why. Because they're pretty."

Then he asked me how old I was, where I'd come from, what I was majoring in. My answers were "Um," "Well," and "I'm not sure." I really liked him and he was making me sweat.

"Just let me know if these questions are too hard."

"I guess I'm nineteen," I said. I thought this over. "That is, I'm sure I am."

While Mark ate half my unburger and all of his, we decided we would go to a movie that weekend. He took my hand and we went to the cashier to pay. While we were waiting in line, he reached for the bowl of pastel mints on the counter, and, with one hand, deftly opened his pocket and poured half the bowl of mints into the pocket. I tried to pretend I didn't know him, but this was difficult since we were still holding hands. When we got into his car—a Spitfire about fifteen years old—I sneezed and he reached inside his jacket for a napkin.

I blew my nose. "Do you always do that?" I said.

"Offer a lady my handkerchief?"

"Take napkins and mints from the restaurant."

"It depends how broke I am." He laughed. "Of course, I'm always broke, so I guess the answer to the question is yes." He looked at me closely. "You know what? I like you. I like you so much I'll tell you what. I'm going to mend my ways. That's what my grandmother always used to tell me, 'You mend your ways, young man.' And now I'm going to take her advice." He counted all his napkins and mints. "Twenty-seven napkins and forty-four mints. Write that down. I'll pay them back when I get some money, probably sometime in my next life. You can keep track for me." He smiled his buoyant smile, and I felt challenged by the sarcasm in it. Then he laughed—he knew I was entertained.

Back at my house the pale purple flowers on the jacaranda tree looked white in the night. The sky was red from a fire in some hills but the wind blew in the opposite direction so we could barely smell the smoke. Mark stared at the back of his hands. Maybe they fascinated him as much as they fascinated me. "Sometimes I can't believe these are my hands," he said. "They look like they belong to somebody older, somebody different." Neither of us said anything else for a while. I think Mark was sort of like me sometimes. Sometimes, I couldn't think what to say so I didn't talk, but other times the reason I didn't always respond right away was that it took me a second to figure things out. We sat quietly, sort of figuring things out. Nothing in particular, just figuring. The wind started to change and we could smell smoke. "So what made you go back to school?" said Mark. I told him about being in the hospital, and he seemed to understand. He was silent, and I saw the seriousness beneath the buoyancy. He looked at my arm, and I felt as if he could see my scars through my sweater sleeve. I was torn between pulling up my sleeve and showing him, or pulling my arm away. I pulled up my sleeve. The muscles in my right arm had adhered to the inner layer of skin, so that every time my hand moved, the forearm skin squirmed. The arm had unusual indentations and curves, and you could see the spot where the hand and arm had become almost separate. The hair on my right arm had grown darker and longer than the hair on my left arm while I was in a cast, and my right wrist was less graceful than the left. Everything was still a little red, not healed yet.

After the accident, I'd thought about this very day, when I first showed my injury to a man. In my fantasies the man said, "Oh, Francie, that doesn't matter," and then we started to talk about something else and my arm was forgotten. Mark reached out to touch me but I must have cringed a little and he pulled back, all the time looking curiously at my arm. Then he did what everyone I liked and thought was well mannered did. He started to talk of other things, but because he was curious and lively he studied my arm when he thought I wasn't looking, and because I was trying to be polite, I stayed very still when I knew he was looking, so as not to embarrass him. And in the end it was the way I'd pictured it, not mattering at all.

"What about you?" I said after a silence. "What are you doing in school?"

He figured a moment. "When I was a kid and I used to talk back to my parents, they would say you never knew when your life was going to peak, or when it was starting to level out at the place where you'd never climb any higher. They said sometimes it happens when you're older or middle-aged, but usually it happens much, much younger. My dad used to say, 'It could happen tomorrow, maybe it happened yesterday. So don't be so smug.' Then he'd punch my face in." I can't explain how that answered my question, but I felt it did.

The next day, the wind had changed completely and my car was covered with ash, as were all the bungalow's windows. The sky was medium-deep gray, and the air smelled heavily of fire. Many of the jacaranda's flowers had come loose in the night. Maybe they'd suffocated from the smoke. They'd fallen in the shape of the tree, a lilac shadow beneath the jacaranda. All day at the city room, everybody complained about the ash, but I thought it was cool, the way something from so far away had come so close and settled over all of us.

Family Man

Because Auntie continued to make deliveries to the motel, the owner allowed her to keep the same room we'd always used. Besides, the place never filled up, except with an occasional mini-convention of cult members who thought aliens were about to land in the desert, things like that. I accompanied my aunt on one delivery. We asked the motel owner and his family whether they remembered anything more than they'd already told Auntie that might help us find Rohn. They said there was nothing they could remember. I didn't know whether that meant there was nothing they could remember, or nothing they could say. Probably the for-

mer. A lot of people couldn't help trying to forget things it might
be dangerous to know. No one had seen Max the Magician in
weeks, though a couple of times there was food missing from
the kitchen. Max began to take on a mythic importance in my
mind, as did the desert. Max and the desert were our last links
to Rohn.

The motel owner told us that Rohn had mentioned a "mys-
terious mission" to him once, and that set us to thinking. Rohn,
however, had always possessed an aptitude for exaggerating, so
we didn't take this mission business too seriously. We'd kept
everything in the motel room the same, in case the room "called"
him home, but we decided now to look through his belongings
for hints of what might have happened to him. The room, which
used to have a certain off-center homeyness, now seemed abandoned and scary. Annie had not thought to look through his
things because she assumed he had no secrets worth noting. In
his papers we found Christmas cards from plumbers and notes
like "Use smoke in the Green Room" and "Don't fill the bottle"
that had to do with a board game he played sometimes. "Mys-
terious mission" was written on one such note, so that's where
that came from. Thinking everybody kept secrets worth noting,
I was surprised to find that he kept none at all. Auntie had
already searched his things at home. She'd felt guilty about it
but there was nothing left for her to do. But it was a waste of
time because any secrets of Rohn's were in his head, not in his
filing cabinets, not in the closets.

I took a break from searching and went outside to sit on my
familiar rock. As I sat out there, I kept imagining Max showing
up the way he often used to. Every time I heard a sound, I took
out my Mace gun and poised to shoot. I was practicing and play-
acting at the same time, like a kid. I'd put my gun away and
at the smallest sound I'd leap to my feet. Across the field, the
trucks never ceased driving. I thought of how once when I

constructed a greenhouse, I decided to buy a few thousand
ladybugs and release them in the greenhouse to control aphids.
I'd held the carton of bugs in my hand and could feel their
movement, a slight uneven vibration in my palm. I placed both
palms around the carton and closed my eyes to feel their life.
When I put my ear near them, I heard them crawling and walking
over one another. When I closed my eyes and heard and felt
them, I felt the difference between their existence and mine.
My perspective altered. Now the vision of and the slight noise
of the trucks seemed to represent an existence as different from
mine as that of the ladybugs'.

Rohn used to play his favorite board game with the same
group of friends every week in Hollywood. Almost always, he
came in second to the same man. He would sit around for hours
wracking his brain trying to come up with new strategies. In
fact, when he was thinking about his game was one of the few
times he wasn't talking. He wanted to win badly because the
man who usually won was a professor at a university, and Rohn
thought he was a pig at the trough of knowledge. "Oink! Oink!
Pedagogy! Oink! Snort! Deconstruction!" he would shout whenever this man had left the house triumphant after a game. Yet
when we'd told this man Rohn was missing, he burst into tears.

Rohn was competitive in other ways, as I was. Once, we
made a bet about how many people patronized a certain grocery
store on an average late night and early morning, and we stayed
up all night in the truck, keeping count of how many people
came and went. At some point I said sleepily that I gave up,
but he said no, that he wanted me to witness whatever happened.
He lost, but he tried to con me into thinking I'd lost by saying
we shouldn't have included any customers after five a.m.

"But we said seven a.m. when we made the bet," I said.
"Pay up, Rohnny, or I'm suing."

But somehow all his faults and conning added up to a great

guy. Maybe it was because he cared so *much* about the things and people he cared about. Or because he was an outlaw and a family man at the same time.

The desert field was cool and windy. I heard a loud scrape and I leaped up with my gun poised, sure it was Max. It was Auntie.

"Sorry, did I scare you?" she said.

"It's okay."

"What are you thinking about?"

"Rohn, of course."

She sat uncertainly on another rock, and I chuckled to myself. Auntie did not look natural sitting on a rock. Presently I heard a series of throat noises emanating from her. "I've done everything I can do. But I feel I should try to do even more so maybe I'll get arrested and I can find out for sure what happened to him."

I felt panicky. "Don't do that! What if they arrest you but still don't tell you anything?"

"I just want to yell at somebody. There's nobody to yell at. There's nobody to talk to, and nobody seems to know anything. What does it take to break through?"

I turned my face skyward and half yelled, half howled, "Uncle Rohn." My aunt howled, too, and in a second we were both howling "Rohn" like madwomen, just to get it out of our systems.

We were making such a ruckus the motel owner came out with an AZ-100 rifle to see what was wrong. I ran over to talk to him.

"What's going on out there? Did you see Rohn?"

"No, we were calling for him, just to get it out of our systems."

"Scared the life out of my family."

"I'm sorry, we weren't thinking."

"You oughta think more." But he was already relaxing. "I know it's hard." He lowered his voice. "I lost someone myself once."

"I never knew that. Who was it?"

"A brother. He showed up later, though, in a couple of years."

"Where had he been?"

"He wasn't sure. He was arrested and transferred to various jails and charged with breaking the Consumption Law. They had it all documented, how much he'd spent and where he'd spent it in the last five years. Then one day they let him go. Why I don't know. What was the question? Oh, he doesn't know where he was. He *thought* it was around here because he *thought* he could hear a rumbling from the highway that he *thought* was the trucks."

"What does he do now?"

"Works for the San Mateo County government. He used to do delivery, like you guys. Once a week or so I get a call or letter from him. Before he was arrested, he called me maybe three times a year. But we were close, we loved each other. We just weren't demonstrative. Now we're more demonstrative, but I don't feel as close to him."

"Well," I said doubtfully. "At least it's the county. The county's always the best, if you're going to work for government."

Auntie let loose again: "Rohn, Rohn!" She stretched out each call so that it wavered and changed pitch. It was the only noise I could hear, drowning out the vague noise of the trucks. But during the breaks in her calls, the familiar low rumble was the only sound.

When we returned to Los Angeles, my aunt decided that she was going to sell or rent her bungalow. I understood. When Rohn had lived with us, I never even noticed, for instance, the walls in the dining room. But now that he was gone, whenever

I was eating, my eyes couldn't help but be drawn to the cracks lining the walls. Even my plants sometimes began to seem inert rather than full of life. I still loved them, but I needed a vacation from their demands. Besides, I knew that when I moved I wouldn't have enough space or light to care for them properly.

There was a place I knew where I might be able to sell all the plants. It was a huge, messy nursery in Silverlake, a mess just like one I hoped to have someday if I ever ran a nursery. It had been a long time since I'd bought any plants there, since I usually propagated from what I had. The nursery was run out of the home of an old Asian couple. You couldn't see into the store. The view was blocked by a bamboo fence, and as high as the fence was, hundreds of oldham bamboos behind it reached higher, as high as fifty feet. One freak bamboo was more than sixty feet tall, with a six-inch diameter. While many bamboos will grow several feet a day during their growth period, the woman who ran this nursery had told me her tallest bamboo once grew ten feet in one day.

Once, when I'd been buying a palm at the nursery, I saw the woman paying for some plants from a friend who was moving. If the friend came back, he could repurchase his plants. It was sort of like a plant pawn shop. The owner seemed to have unlimited resources, but that wasn't possible, because nobody has unlimited resources.

Auntie and I took as many of my plants as would fit in the truck. When we walked through the front gate, about fifteen small dogs ran up yapping and nipping at our calves. A small, middle-aged man—the owner's husband—ran up saying, "Shoo, shoo." At first I thought he was talking to Auntie and me, not to the dogs.

"I'm sorry," he said to us. "They don't seem to remember you. Are you still raising plants?"

"Actually, I came to sell some. They're very well grown, but my aunt and I are moving into apartments and won't really be able to take care of them properly anymore."

"My wife's not home. You wait." He gestured with his hand toward the huge garden in front, and turned and walked away. We strolled through the messy, beautiful grounds. Bamboo roots stuck up in bumps from the earth, and there were dozens of bamboo stumps—the fence accounted for that. Large goldfish swam through greenish water among the water hyacinths and the dwarf cattails, which looked like very thin stalks of green onions.

When the woman who ran the nursery arrived, she brought along her mother. Both women were tiny, but the mother was as small as a child. I told them about my plants.

"Come in, come in," said the younger woman, indicating that I should follow her. She took us into a parlor in which one whole wall was covered with staghorn ferns, hanging like trophies from a hunt.

"Did you want to see my plants?" I said.

"Oh, of course. Of course I'll buy them. I'm sure they're wonderful." She poured us some tea. "Drink, drink, drink, drink." Then she mumbled to herself, "Drink, drink."

Her mother suddenly spat out, "Drink, drink," in a falsetto singsong. I turned to her and she wrinkled her nose and made a funny face.

"Now, why are you selling your plants?" said the daughter.

I explained how we were planning to move from the house. She pulled out an enormous wad of bills and said, "How many plants are there?"

"Including the ones still at home, maybe seventy."

"Seventy or eighty, and each of them a gem," said Auntie, the bargainer.

The woman counted out some money and handed it to me. "Is that enough?"

"But you haven't seen the plants yet."

"I'm sure they'll be lovely. Now, tell me, what are you doing with yourself if not raising plants?"

"I'm going to school. I have a boyfriend named Mark."

The mother started to chant "Drink, drink" again.

I said, "It feels weird not to have to ride to richtown all the time anymore."

The mother said in her singsong voice, "Drink, drink. When richtown falls, there will be lots to drink. First, less to drink, then there will be more."

There was something about her singsongy voice, something about how tiny she was. She made me think. I thought of richtown as someplace that had always been there and always would, like the blue sky and the hills. But wasn't the sky less blue every day? And who could see the hills in the smog? I knew she *knew*. She had seen it in her head, the fate of richtown.

"So what do you suggest I do?" I said.

"Grow your plants, or don't grow your plants. Go to school, or don't go to school. Fall in love, or don't fall in love. That's my advice," she said.

"But if everything is going to be changing?"

"If, if, if," she sang.

"Before you said *when* richtown falls."

She looked behind herself for a moment. "Talking to me? Did I say 'when'? You're young. Be young. That's my advice."

Auntie Annie tugged on my sleeve and suggested we bring the plants in. She hated it when I got involved talking to people like this woman or like Max the Magician, people she found mystic, and, therefore, possibly evil. We brought the plants in, but then I saw some plants I loved, so I bought two. I figured apartments in Los Angeles, even the most cramped ones, usually had balconies, even if the balcony was only half a foot wide. I could put plants on my future balcony, or right inside the glass balcony door. But I got only two because I had the feeling I wanted to be traveling light for a while.

My aunt walked back to the truck but I remained for a moment to talk to the old woman. "When do I stop being young?" I asked.

"If you have to ask, maybe you've already stopped." She chuckled with delight. "Stop, stop," she said.

I felt very excited. She'd rarely talked to me before, usually just sitting staring at walls or something. I'd always thought she was a great, scary person. I thought she too had known things as a child.

"My aunt's man is missing," I said, eagerly. "Do you know where he went?"

"He'll come back," she said. "You'll find him."

"He'll come back or I'll find him. Which is it?"

Her son-in-law was sitting watching TV. Her daughter was listening pleasantly to us. The mother started to answer my question but suddenly I had a fit. My nose tickled. I sneezed repeatedly, my all-time record of twenty sneezes in a row. I know because I counted, having nothing else to think about while I had my fit. When I finished, the old lady was smiling serenely at a plant.

"Excuse me, I didn't hear you," I said, but she didn't turn from the plant. I thought, irrationally, that she'd given me that fit. She was a miracle lady, like Max was a miracle, and like, in a different way, I'd always thought of my parents as miracles.

I started to lose control of my mouth. I decided I needed to tell her about Rohn, about Mark, about plants, about the paper at school. I blabbered on, though I could hear my aunt calling to me and though the old woman never turned to look at me. But I knew she was listening. My lips and tongue were moving fast. I saw a couple of bits of saliva fly like sparks from my mouth. When I stopped talking, I felt relaxed, ready to go home. I turned and left, feeling the old woman's eyes on my back as I walked out of the room.

Jewel

Jewel, who I figured was in her late thirties, liked to wear tight dresses, often with polka dots, from about a decade ago, in the early forties. The dresses were sometimes stained and torn, but they were pretty, or at least they had been. Mark said Jewel was stuck in a clothes warp, wearing clothes from the time she was happiest. Precisely, that was 2042, and she was between boyfriends. At the same time that she was buying those dresses, I was nine. What I mainly remembered from then was that my family lived on the fourth floor of an apartment in Chicago, and I used to look out the window and see windmills and solar panels on the rooftops of the buildings all around. During warm, windy summer nights, when I kept my windows open, I could hear the soft *whirr* of the windmills, so unlike the scrape above the city room.

Jewel liked to sit around telling us stories from when she herself was nine. She said that when she, her brothers, and sisters behaved especially badly, their mother would cry as she beat them. Jewel wasn't sure what her mother cried over, but in bed at night she and her siblings would think not about the beatings but about the crying. "Our mother didn't *want* to beat us," Jewel would tell us. Her father never beat them exactly, but rather swatted them across the room when he was mad— just one hard shove with his forearm and they went flying. And then he wasn't mad anymore.

Neither of her parents was the cause of her crooked nose. That was from an old boyfriend, from before she started the journalism program five years earlier. Now and then over time, this boyfriend still appeared in her life, or perhaps he never really left. Jewel said it was like going to a house where you used to live and looking at it from the outside. A part of you still feels it's yours. So in that way she still felt this man was hers, and she, his.

There were two stories that dominated our time at school. One was about a student, Matt Burroughs, who was accused of killing someone during a robbery. He said he'd just been passing by when the robbery occurred. Though he'd been convicted, he was released on appeal. We decided to be a crusading newspaper and help free Burroughs, who many people thought was innocent. Burroughs was a safe cause for us. Murder, unlike black-market buying and selling, or violence by political protestors, was considered a crime against individuals, not against the state.

There was a sweetness to Matt that made us want to fall all

thetical situations, but Matt had the confidence of knowing that his sweetness would almost always determine his behavior. Jewel said, "I'd be sweet too if a bunch of people were trying to set me free after I'd killed someone." But she believed in him in the end.

The other story mainly belonged to Bernard. He'd been doing an article about how some of the male athletes at the college worked as prostitutes, and through this story, he began to suspect that an administrator at the school patronized these students, possibly in exchange for grades or parking passes.

Otherwise, most of the stories were on things like rising parking fees and grant deadlines. That was the sort of story I got assigned, because I was new.

Our campus was larger than a high school but possessed none of the sprawling vibrance of the universities I'd seen. All the buildings were straight, square, squat. There were about twenty thousand students, averaging in their early thirties. The majority were there for vocational training. Every day, something was happening on the quad: marches or demonstrations, clubs selling baked goods, petitioners screaming at you like preachers. Everything was glazed over by hazy sunlight.

Vendors lined the street in front of the campus, selling books and pizzas and soft drinks. Behind them were stores: College Books, College Sub, College Drugstore. Bland stores, a little seedy. On the side streets stood beat-up stucco houses protected by noisy dogs of no special breed. And way to the north, you could see the Hollywood Hills on rare clear days.

Once, a student ran for City Council and called a press conference. There were balloons and hundreds of press kits, but I was the only one who showed up. I asked him and his press aide a few questions and left, walking out of the darkened auditorium into the sun. I was surprised by how light it was, and how dark the auditorium had been—often, the sun seeped into every crack and touched everything with its heat. I turned around and saw the student and his aide leaving the auditorium, struggling to carry their press kits and balloons. Later, for the election, there was an eight percent turnout, and the student won. Several years earlier, protestors had organized to encourage people *not* to vote, but there was a backlash and fifty-seven percent turned out. Since then, voting patterns for local elections had returned to normal.

Jewel was the managing editor of the paper, and Bernard, the editor. I never trusted Bernard, but Mark's friend Lucas said he was all right, and that just because he always acted guilty didn't mean he'd actually done anything wrong. I hardly talked to anyone except Mark and sometimes Lucas and Jewel. Lucas never took off his tie and sometimes kept his suit jacket on even during warm weather. He said he'd once shaved his head, as most radical blacks had several years earlier, but today it had all grown out and hung in a neat braid down his back. The suit and hair were part of his discipline. Wearing a suit wasn't such a jump from his old life—everybody in his gang had been extremely disciplined, too. I asked him what "disciplined" meant and he said, "You could stick a knife in some of them and they wouldn't change expression." Sometimes when my right arm got stiff, he helped me do exercises with it. He was the only person I knew who could do this well, because he was the only one who didn't get scared that he might hurt me. Mark and my aunt refused to be anything but extremely gentle with my arm, even if they knew being firm was for my own good. Mark said he would be able to help if I were just a friend. Sometimes as Lucas stretched my arm, the pain would cause tears to fall from my eyes, and I could tell how hard it was for him even though he never changed expression; or rather I knew precisely *because* he never changed expression.

house, which Auntie had finally rented out. I knew that my life
literally had started with my birth, but in a way, I thought my
life was just beginning in earnest then. I took out the old notebooks in which I'd scribbled notes from my parents' hospital
talks and packed them with my most important items. I didn't
actually plan to reread them, but they'd taken on a symbolic
importance now that I was moving out. They represented everything that was in my brain that I would need to draw on in the
future.

Before I left, I pried a board from the back porch to take
with me in case I never lived in Auntie's house again. Auntie
and I didn't want to get all dramatic, yet we felt upset to be
separating. So we stayed up all night playing cards—normal,
boring gin rummy—just to be doing something together on our
last night.

I'd saved some money and now worked part-time with a
lawyer, and Mark said I could always find more money
somewhere.

I worked for what I guess you'd have to call a sleazebag
lawyer, although I liked him. He'd been disbarred for several
years for bribing the wrong person, but recently he'd been re-
admitted to the bar after bribing the right person. His glasses
were broken and he used to walk around the office with a huge
rubber band around his head to hold one of the lenses in. But
whenever clients came in, he took off his glasses and sat there
squinting across his desk. Every time he bagged a new client,
he would be filled with self-doubts in a way that I found quite
existential. He couldn't decide if the clients were just stupid or
if maybe he really could help them. With his rubber band around
his head, he would pace his office saying, "Can I really help
them? Can I?"

Before I moved out, Lucas and I helped Mark with one of
his latest money-making schemes. He'd been on his own since

he was fourteen, so he'd learned to be an opportunist. Someone
he knew had owned a uniform store near UCLA, but the store
had gone out of business. His friend told him he could take the
fixtures, so we went out to get them. It was a Saturday night,
and there were students all over going to movies or restaurants.
They were in such a different world from me that I barely noticed
them. We were like different species.

At first, Mark's keys to the shop didn't work and Lucas got
nervous that an alarm would go off, sort of reflexive nervousness
left over from when he was committing crimes as a kid. "She
said there's no alarm," said Mark, right before an alarm
sounded. "Help, you're hurting me," said the mechanical voice
in a loud, bored tone. But the voice turned off after Mark figured
out the keys and got the door open.

Inside, we found a lot of hangers, a pink metal-and-glass
chest, and eight pink doors. We'd parked several blocks away
and had to carry the doors two by two to the car. "These doors
must be worth a thousand bucks apiece," said Mark. "Doors
are expensive." Mark knew the cost of everything.

"Yeah, but what does a guy do with thousands of dollars
worth of pink doors?" said Lucas.

"I'll bet my aunt would like one," I said. "She likes pink."

"I'll give her one, then." Mark spoke with his usual buoyancy, as well as his usual trace of sarcasm. "I want to buy love
with my largesse."

Once, as we were walking, a police car stopped along the
curb and drove slowly next to us for about two blocks. Finally
one of the officers said, "May I ask what you're doing? I mean,
don't let me bother you or anything, but what the hell are you
doing?"

"We have to take these doors to the car," said Mark. He
kept pulling on one end of the doors while Lucas and I tried

The policeman turned to his partner, who was driving, and said, "Oh, of *course*, they have to take the doors to the car." I remembered Rohn and the highway patrolmen who'd been shining flashlights in our truck. I handed the weight of our end of the door to Lucas and reached into my wallet for some water creds. I didn't know how much was appropriate. We really hadn't done anything. I handed them two low-denomination creds. The officer mumbled something and both policemen studied us for a moment before they drove on.

"They sure make me nervous," said Lucas.

"Not me. It's hard to scare me," I said. "Wah! A moth," I said, waving one frantically away.

"There's a lot of cops around tonight," said Mark. He nodded at another police car.

"There's always a lot around, you're just noticing them now," said Lucas. "I notice them all the time."

There was really only one moment when I felt fully aware of our surroundings—girls and boys with tank tops, tanned arms, and blond hair, majoring in psych or poli-sci or business. And here we were carrying pink doors. But the moment passed.

"Pay attention," snapped Mark, just as I tumbled over a crack in the sidewalk. The doors we were carrying fell on Mark's feet.

"Oh, sorry," I said. "You're not hurt?"

He frowned, then smiled. "That's okay, I've always wanted a limp. It's more dramatic."

We made three trips between the shop and Mark's apartment. He lived in a small place, and we just stacked everything on the bare floor. At one point a door had fallen off the car, but otherwise everything went fine. When we drove to my place to move me out of the house, we brought Auntie a door, which she declared "simply lovely," but she seemed a little perplexed. She said the people who would be renting the house had called today to offer to buy it. She turned them down, but I could tell she was still considering it. She could sell it for a lot more than she would report, so she wouldn't have to pay taxes on the profit, and the buyer wouldn't have to pay high property taxes. That's the way everybody east of richtown made large transactions. You carried a gun and took a second with you because so much cash changed hands.

I wanted her to rent, not sell. I thought if she did away with too many memories of her life with Rohn, she would do away with Rohn himself.

Auntie sat on the back porch while Mark, Lucas, and I loaded stuff and I did some last-minute packing. Once, Mark picked up a towel. "Are you taking this?"

"That's my good towel. I never touch that towel unless I've washed my hands first." He looked at me patiently. "I have this thing about towels," I said.

He and Lucas exchanged the same look they'd exchanged when they first met me. He picked up a necklace. "What about this?"

"Be careful, that thing's bad luck. I was wearing it when Rohn disappeared, but I'm afraid to throw it away." I felt earnest and sheepish at the same time.

"Can I touch this?" said Mark sarcastically, pointing to a pillow.

"Of course," I said, annoyed. "Why couldn't you?"

After we'd unloaded everything at my new apartment, we dropped Lucas off and started to set up my place much the way my bedroom at home had been set up. Actually, the apartment was about the same size as my bedroom. Across the way, an immense flag flew over a used-car lot. The newer cars were sleek and rounded, almost balloonlike, the older ones oddly rectangular. A spotlight behind the flag threw a huge rippling shadow across my ceiling and wall. Mark and I lay in bed watching the shadow of the flag ripple above us. It was almost like a strobe light as we had sex. I think the light, and the unfamiliarity of the room, lent a striking and exciting impersonality to our love-making. I felt free of a lot of obligations, free of my girlishness. After sex, I was always refreshed, he was always tired. For the first time, I didn't mind the way he fell asleep with fatigue. In fact, I was very moved by his sleeping face as light flicked back and forth across him.

Mark needed to leave at four a.m., as he often did. He worked part-time unloading groceries. Whenever he woke up for middle-of-the-night work, his face held a grimness that contrasted with the face I saw as he was drifting off to sleep. Those drifting periods were the most relaxed I ever saw him, more relaxed even in those early moments of sleep than in mid-sleep, when he often seemed tense.

I felt lonely after he'd left. I'd never been alone like that before, in a place of my own. I was afraid I might get used to it.

Late one Wednesday night when Jewel had had too much to drink, she told anyone who would listen that the problem between men and women was that for men sex was like violence, and for women it was like food. I thought sex was more like water, the way it could be very hard or very soft, or spread all over or concentrated in one place. I got up and hung a sheet across the window and got back in bed, but now the flag shadow rippled across the sheet. Blouses lay and hung all over the place, small white ghosts in the dark. A cousin named Steven who'd lived with us for a while when I was eleven used to be terrified of ghosts. I'd read that that fear was increasingly common among children, even children from small towns and wealthy families.

Though we weren't together long, I got attached to Steven, who was a few years younger than I was, and his seventeen-year-old sister, Nadine, who also stayed with us. While they stayed with us, my mother had worked in downtown Chicago for a pearl company. Sometimes, when she didn't have a night class at the college she was attending, Steven and I would go down to her office and watch women with lightning fingers stringing pearls. Afterward, we three would ride home on the el train together. We lived at the end of the line, at Howard Street. I used to love the ride. I loved the names of some of the stations: Addison and Division and Armitage—crisp, sharp, angular names; Sheridan and Diversey and Thorndale—cool, tough names; Morse and Jarvis and Howard—solid names, unadorned names. From the windows of the el, I could see the back porches of hundreds of brick apartments, and now and then between the apartments, I could see Lake Michigan, bluer than the sky during summer, blacker during winter when we rode home in darkness. Steven's parents had been broke and receiving threats from loan sharks. But when they got back on their feet, my cousins left, Steven to his home, and Nadine to her own place. I had fallen in love with them, but we rarely saw each other again. Their parents divorced and Steven went to live with his mother, who was not a blood relative of mine. That was one of the first empty spots in my heart, but it was a small one compared to what would follow.

I had just fallen asleep when the phone rang. I'd forgotten to turn off the voice for bedtime, and the phone recited the caller's number: 674-8430. I didn't recognize the number, but I figured it was Mark calling from work.

"Hello?"

"Francie? It's Jewel. I got your number from your aunt. Sorry. I woke her up."

"What's wrong?"

"Nothing. How is everything with you?"

"With me? Why? Has something happened?"

"Oh, no. I'm sorry, I know it's late." Her voice was eager,

with a bit of forced easiness. It was odd, because usually she was so flippant. "I was just wondering if you would do me a favor."

"What is it?"

The shadow from the flag was still flickering. I turned on the light. Ghosts, shadows disappeared. Just a big mess—boxes, books, and clothes—remained. I could hear traffic noises over the phone. "Are you okay? Where are you?"

"Just down the street actually." I'd told her where I was moving.

"What's the favor?" I asked again.

"I have to go bail a friend out of jail, and I was wondering if you would come with me. I don't want to go alone." I hesitated from sleepiness. "Also, I guess I just want him to think I have friends." Her voice cracked. I could scarcely believe it was Jewel, she seemed so different, so unsure of herself.

I said okay. It made sense to me when stuff like this happened. Sometimes things that should not have made sense to me did, and things that should have made sense did not. Now and then, I could look at an ordinary chair or tree and feel confused, and then later I could see five ambulances in a row speeding down Western Avenue and this made perfect sense. Certainly it was not out of the ordinary. I was always asking people things like, "What would you do if I suddenly disappeared?" or "What would you do if I started screaming at the top of my lungs? Would that surprise you?" And I guess what I was really asking was, "Is the world as wiggly for you as it is for me?" Once, the Frog Club cook from House of Burgers asked me what I would do if I looked in the mirror one morning and I'd become someone else, someone large and pale instead of small and dark. I said I probably wouldn't be too surprised, because sometimes I was sort of out of touch with reality. He said, "That's the part of us that's compatible!" Anyway, it made sense to me that someone I didn't know well would call me up in the middle of the night to help her bail someone I didn't know at all out of jail. In fact, a couple of times when I was little my parents had needed to bail people out of jail and I'd gone with them because it was too late to get a sitter. Once, my father had even had to bail out my mother. The fear that someone you knew would be arrested was pervasive in most communities, but the fear became just another part of your life, like, say, arthritis becomes part of the larger life of an arthritic. You still have to eat, work, walk, talk, sleep, love.

Jewel was at my door in a few minutes. I'd fallen back asleep and she pounded on the door instead of knocking. She was already talking when I opened the door. "The motor's running. It's a false charge, grand theft or something, and he just doesn't want to spend the night there. Also I have to go to a bank machine. I need money for the bail bondsman." She often gestured with her hands, and there was always something dramatic about her. Her clear voice had now taken on a slight bray from excitement.

The bondsman's business was near the jail, which was in the San Fernando Valley. He himself was driving in all the way from where he lived twenty miles away. "An old boyfriend," she said. "But he won't take a check for the ten." I learned later that meant for the ten percent of the bail that the bondsman received as his fee. Jewel wanted to take out the limit from the bank machine, but she didn't have that much in her account. She put her hand impatiently on the scanner to restart the transaction. "Please try again, Julia," said the machine. I hadn't known that was her name. I didn't like it at all. To me, she was Jewel.

After she got her money, we caught the freeway. Everyone I knew hated the freeways. I liked them at night, the way they were sort of black-green with a hint of blue like water, and the

way you moved so softly on them. I imagined I could see a heat
trail behind the cars, like the trail boats leave in the water.
Though I hadn't asked, I knew it was Jewel's ex-boyfriend, the
one who'd beaten her up, in jail. Partly I could tell by how eager
she was. Years earlier, in Chicago, I'd spent the summer with
the family of my best friend, Lily. Her father beat up her mother
a number of times, and at first my friend and I reacted sort of
the way Jewel was: we tried twice as hard to please him. Every
time he hit her, we would clean the house. We didn't yet know
whether the beatings were her mother's shame or her father's.
We'd scrub the kitchen floor, examine it with pride, and wait
hopefully for the moment when Lily's father might walk in and
see what we'd done. We used to love television commercials,
because they all seemed to be telling you that something could
be achieved, that if you bought their special medicine to make
you stop sneezing, you would be one step higher on the evo-
lutionary trail. That's what we were doing when we used to clean
up—we were trying to achieve this higher, happier state. I know
it's ridiculous to say, but in our worst hours, television commercials really comforted us.

Tall buildings loomed suddenly to our left, their corporate
logos shining above them. I adjusted my glasses, which were
held together with masking tape and which I normally never
wore in public.

When we got to the Valley, the bondsman hadn't arrived
yet. Jewel got out and called him on the twenty-four-hour direct
line in front of his business. Because we were near the jail,
there were several bail bond places around, and a few were
open. A girl working in the place across the road eyed us and
waved us over. But Jewel said they all required property as
collateral. This guy here was just doing her a favor. Next door
was an X-rated store. From the open doorway I saw a mousey
man reading *Glamour* magazine, which more men read than

women, to look at the naked girls. I went to sit in the car by myself. The street was wide and empty. The light changed and a car drove by, whipping up pieces of garbage in its wake. I slid over and opened the car door to pick up a flyer from the street. It had my name on it. It said Francesca the Magnificent could tell your fortune and give you advice about business, love, and family. I put the flyer in my pocket. We might need it. Who could tell what the evening would come to?

When the bondsman arrived, Jewel and I went inside. She asked him whether a lot of people called him on his direct line, but he said hardly ever. "Once in a while they wake me up, but it's part of the business. I hardly ever come out even if they do call. It's never worth my time." His face became wistful. "But a part of you keeps waiting for that big call, that five-million-dollar bail." As he talked and filled out forms, he looked toward Jewel every so often, as if maybe he'd been in love with her once but wasn't anymore, though he was still curious.

He said he was going home to sleep for a few hours after he helped us, and then he'd open up shop again. He asked me to promise him I would "make Jewel make what's-his-name come by later to have his picture taken and sign some papers." Jewel paid the ten percent, and then she put her arms around her stomach and turned away, looking sick. He hesitated before taking the money, but he took it anyway. That's why I liked him, because he hesitated, and then he took it anyway. I hoped that's what I would have done in the same situation. I hoped that if someone ever broke my heart, as perhaps she had his, I would never forget how it felt to be in love with him, so I would do him a favor, but I would also have enough self-respect to put out my hand and say, "Pay me what you owe me."

He reached into a shoebox on the counter and gave Jewel and me key-card holders that said "Sam Shapiro's Bail Bonds —We Care" on them. He pointed at the chains, then at us. "I mean it," he said. "You know who to bring your business to next time." He spoke as if reciting, and when he was done talking, he relaxed and his face looked haggard. We locked up with him, and then watched his car rush off down the wide empty street.

"Come on," I said. Jewel shook herself—she'd been staring after the car.

"He has five kids now," she said.

"He's nice."

She shook her head, as if to clear her mind. "We've got to hurry."

The jail was a bland place, lit with fluorescent light, reminiscent of a principal's office at a grammar school. Jewel had put on lipstick right before we went in. The officer at the reception desk would let only one of us through to the interior, so Jewel walked back with the bail envelope. I sat on a wooden bench. It was four thirty, and no one else was around. There were a couple of signs saying visitors were being monitored, as well as scanned for metal, though I didn't see any cameras or scanners. On a far wall hung twelve framed moving photographs of officers. The photographs weren't plugged in, thank goodness. That trend had come and gone quickly. I hated moving photographs, watching someone smile over and over again all day. The officers on the wall were in various states of smiles and half-smiles. They were men and women from that precinct who'd been killed over the years. The oldest picture was from the twenties; the newest, of a very young man, was from a few weeks earlier. It was funny how not only their haircuts but also the looks in their faces seemed to fit their different eras. Maybe, in some weird way, we all fit in exactly where we were, even if we didn't feel like it sometimes.

The man at the desk, who said his name was Officer Tom, asked me what I was in for and winked. He was gray-haired, with a paunch and a well-meaning face. His gun hung at his side as he worked at cutting strips of paper with scissors and inserting them into brochures.

"It's a tough job but somebody's got to do it," he said, but he seemed embarrassed.

"I like cutting paper," I babbled, suddenly incredibly sleepy. "It's very relaxing, like sewing a hem. It's mindless, but I feel like I've accomplished something. And I like the sound. I like listening to sounds. I mean some sounds. Not all of them . . . I don't like to sew, actually."

"Interesting." I thought he was just being polite. I did notice, though, that he started cutting with more gusto.

I pulled myself up to peek down the hall where Jewel had vanished. To my surprise, she was sitting only about thirty feet away on a bench just like mine. She grimaced at me and mouthed something I couldn't understand. Every so often, someone had come into the jail and Officer Tom let them go back where Jewel was, but only once had the person come out with somebody else.

I sat down again and didn't say anything for a while.

"Ouch," said Officer Tom. He licked his finger. "Almost lost a digit," he said, smiling. "Cat got your tongue?"

I roused myself and tried to think of something to say. I said, "If you cut off a finger, are you still exactly the same person?" A lens popped out of my glasses and I put it back in. I noticed my pajama pants sticking out of the bottom of my pants.

Finally Jewel joined me. I silently questioned her and she shrugged. She opened up a small case of eye shadow and frowned in the mirror. She was wearing a lot of shimmery gold on her eyelids. That was a richtown affectation. "Isn't this a pretty color?" she said. "I used to steal this same color from the

drugstore all the time when I was a kid. I couldn't steal enough
of it. At one time I had enough to last me for years."

"Before Neiman Marcus went out of business, I stole a scarf
from there once," I said. "When I got home I felt so scared I
was going to get arrested, I stuck the scarf down my pants to
hide it. I kept that scarf stuck down my pants for a week, and
then finally I took it out and left it in a public bathroom somewhere." We giggled.

"How old were you?"

"Ten."

"Yeah, that's when the stealing bug first hits."

Jewel leaned back, eyes closed, lids shining in the fluorescent light. All government buildings used a special type of
fluorescent bulb that lasted for decades, but the bulb faded and
changed tint over time. So everything was slightly purplish in
there. I closed my eyes and listened to the sound of Officer
Tom's scissors cutting paper.

"They say they're processing him, but it's taking forever,"
said Jewel. She sat up and shook my arm. "His name is Teddy.
I know this sounds crazy, but I really do owe him. He really
has come through for me a lot of times."

"Well, you don't owe him anything."

"But I do." She wore a strange expression, fierce, but also
sort of pleading. A few moments earlier, she'd seemed tired,
but now as she spoke about Teddy she seemed energized. "Sometimes he's lent me money when I really needed it, and whenever
I've been desperately unhappy he's put aside what he was doing
to be with me. He has a good heart."

"Stop acting like he's a nice guy," I said, wide awake now.
I didn't like to hear her talk like that about him. We both lay
back again and didn't speak.

"Jewel!" He said it "Jule."

We both came to attention, Jewel standing up and sucking in her stomach audibly.

Because his voice had sounded so big, I'd expected a bigger man, but he was smaller than she was, though strong looking. I admit there was also something vital about him, about his resolute, slightly bow-legged walk, about the way he seemed like someone who could protect you if you needed it. Jewel introduced us and we shook hands. His hand twitched a couple of times in mine, but otherwise his grip was firm. There were certain people who, since my accident, I didn't feel comfortable shaking hands with, as if they might jerk my arm and hurt me. He was one of those people.

The morning was gray, silver gray in the sky, red gray in some brick, pure gray in the streets and sidewalks, grays blending into grays. Everything seemed orderly outside: rectangular patches of grass, square buildings, linear streets. I looked both ways up and down the street. Jewel's car was gone.

We walked along the curb where we knew the car had been parked, examining the area as if for clues. We all three noticed the tow zone sign at the same moment. Jewel and Teddy looked at each other like, Now what? Then Jewel and I looked at each other like, Now what?

We sat for a long time at the bus-stop bench, watching the sun rise over the road, Jewel's arm braided through Teddy's, her hand limp and tired. The bus companies put out schedules, but the buses came whenever they came. Teddy thumped my shoulder with one of his thick hands. The hand twitched a couple of times on my shoulder before he removed it. He spoke with vigor. "Thanks for coming," he said. "Seriously. Thanks." There was something unsettling in his gaze, because maybe he was looking for things about you that you didn't know yourself. And what might he do if he found those things? But he sounded sincere.

As soon as it was seven, Teddy said he needed to make some phone calls, and he walked off to a gas station. It was getting warm, but the colors remained washed out. The streets got more and more crowded. "What do you think?" said Jewel. "Is he what you expected?"

"He's shorter," I said brusquely.

She turned away angrily.

"Jewel, I'm sorry, but I just don't get why you're here helping him."

"Because if I didn't help him, who would?"

And, in a way, that made sense to me, because even if I had a worst enemy, I would bail that enemy out of jail if no one else would. It was the way I was raised to think about jails.

A couple of kids with school notebooks came to wait at the bus stop. "Been waiting long?" one of them said. I nodded, and they got up on the other bench and started pretending they were on a ship scouting for land.

"How old was Raybelle when she made it?" said Jewel, suddenly hopeful. Raybelle was a scientist who'd discovered a cure for a degenerative bone disease. Later, before she died a few years ago, she'd become a popular senator everyone called by her first name.

"You mean got elected to the senate?"

"No, when she started making it as a scientist."

"I'm not sure what you mean by 'making it,' but I think she was in her forties before she started being considered in the top rank of scientists."

"Then I still have a chance."

"For what?"

"Oh, I don't know. To make money, to get famous, to do something that helps people. Anything. Anything."

"Land ahoy!" said one of the kids, seeing the bus.

"You can't say 'ahoy' about land," said the other.

"Ship ahoy, then."

Jewel waved for Teddy, and he hurried over for the bus. I paid my fare, plopped down on a seat, felt something cold and wet seeping up from the cushion. I leaned over and smelled urine and changed seats. During the two-hour bus ride home, the freeway didn't remind me of water anymore. It was just a freeway, already getting congested and filling with exhaust smells and smoke. At the off-ramps, men and boys were selling bags of oranges and cartons of strawberries, but I knew the oranges were dry and the strawberries moldy. I could see young men pushing carts, selling cotton candy and mangoes, hot dogs and balloons. I remembered another time I'd stolen something besides that scarf. I was at a carnival with my parents, who were then quite sick, and a little white girl who was eating cotton candy that I lusted after told me to stop looking at her candy and called me a racial epithet. She carried a shining vinyl purse with her, and I'd grabbed it and shot through the crowd. When I hit an open area, I ran as fast as I could. I heard my mother call my name, and to my surprise, she wasn't yelling at me to stop but to run faster. Ordinarily she was strict with me. "*Run*," she was screaming. It wasn't because the girl had called me a name—my mother hadn't heard that. I'd never been sure what it was, really. Maybe she just hadn't wanted me to get caught, ever. So now I felt that if I was ever caught, the way Jewel was caught, or the way Rohn was caught—any way at all—I would have failed my mother.

Teddy and Jewel slept on each other's shoulders, and once when I turned around, he was stroking her forehead and saying he loved her, which for all I knew was true. But even so, when her stop came I suggested she get off alone. Teddy put up his hands in mock surrender. "Hey, fine with me." She got off before me. He might hit her again someday, but it wouldn't be now, not this morning.

When I got home, Mark was waiting outside my apartment, sitting on the curb. We seemed to do that a lot. His kitchen was so small we always used to eat outside, often sitting at the curb in front of his place.

"There you are. I was worried," he said. "Where were you?"

I snuggled my face into his shirt, smelled his familiar comforting smell. "I met Teddy."

"Jewel's Teddy?"

"Uh-huh. Do you know him?"

"Yeah. He threatened to punch my face in, once."

"How come people keep wanting to punch your face in?"

"You mean that doesn't happen to everyone?" he said. He laughed. "Come on. You can tell me what happened after you have breakfast."

I took a shower upstairs, but when I got out, Mark had left for school and turned down my covers. I hung a blanket up over the sheet on the window and got in bed. It was hard for me to imagine Mark being a little boy and getting beaten up by his parents. My mother never hit me, but she grounded me whenever I hurt something living, even a plant. And at times I definitely was the kind of child who needed to play pranks on animals or to examine insects and their reactions to various types of prodding. I punched my cousin Steven once and my mother grounded me for two weeks; two weeks after that, he was gone.

Possibilities

"I dated a genius once." That was what my friend Lily's mother said one night after her husband beat her up. Her nose was bleeding, and I didn't know why she'd said that, or why she continued talking about this genius. His looks, his straight A's, his name—Minoru—his family. I was seven then, and it was only when I got older that I understood what she was trying to say: Once, there were possibilities.

Lily's grandfather, who'd also beaten her mother years earlier, was what was then called learning impaired. That was why her grandmother chose him, because she could control him except when he was drunk.

Her family had lived in a once-affluent section of Chicago that
then had four types of residents: poor Jews, poor blacks, poor
Asians, and a group of white kids who were at that time considered elite—that was before nonwhites became the majority
in the country. Lily's grandparents had lived near mine but
never met. But our mothers went to school together. I owned a
yearbook of my mother's. The white girls had tried to enlarge
their mouths with lipstick, emulating the naturally full lips of
the black girls. The black girls had straightened their hair to
emulate the naturally straight hair of the Asians. And the Asian
girls wore shadow that rounded out their eyes. All of them looked
quite silly. That had been a strange period of transition in
America.

My mother had three boyfriends in high school. There was
the same smart boy Lily's mother had dated; a boy who was
killed in an auto wreck senior year; and my father, whom she
met at a party given by a girls' club called the Darnells. Hyde
Park is on the South Side, and after my parents got married
they continued living there, near the 43rd Street el station on
the Jackson line. Because my father was half black, half
Chinese, my parents opened up a place called Chu's Chinese
Soul Food. That was where my parents first fell in love, after a
couple of years of marriage. "We used to have sex next to the
rice pots," said my mother. "I could hear all that rice bubbling."
Maybe that's where I was conceived.

When I was born, we moved near the Addison stop, by
Wrigley Field, which the Cubs had just refurbished again. I
could hear but not see the crowds cheering, and when I was
older I'd sit on my front steps with Lily on weekends and watch
crowds pass by after games. I loved the Cubs. I had a crush on
Buster Williams, because his eyes had lustershine, and on Glenn
Williams (no relation), because my Uncle Robin once shook his
hand in a parking lot. Living near Wrigley Field was one of my

favorite things from childhood. Another favorite thing was when my father drove my mother and me up and down Lake Shore Drive, a wonderful fast drive with the bristling skyline to the west and Lake Michigan to the east. The government had already begun the gas cred system, but we didn't drive much and had plenty of creds to take recreational rides once a week. When we drove south, I watched the beach, and when we drove north, I watched the skyscrapers. I always sat behind the driver's seat, and when Steven lived with us, he sat behind the passenger seat. Nadine never came. All the time you could smell the fish and the lake. As we drove so quickly by, I was out there, in that world of beaches and skyscrapers, and not in the car at all. The speed of the car would increase, building, building—seemingly inside me—until finally, my heart pounding, I would say, "*Daddy*, you're going too fast," and he would slow down and I would return to the car: safe.

The other time I rode in a car on Lake Shore Drive was after Lily's parents had divorced and her father took us for a ride with a woman whose hair was piled very high. He opened up his window and the crossbreeze knocked over her hair, which Lily and I thought was God showing his sense of humor. It was a secret between Him and us, so we tried not to giggle but couldn't help it. Her father didn't hit her then, but he wanted to. Perhaps he wanted to hit me, too. So Lily needed to blank out her expression. There were a lot of expressionless people walking around, especially in big cities. They'd learned it in childhood. There was a long time when it seemed to me that violence and death were everywhere I turned, that everyone I knew or had known had been beaten or was being beaten or was dying or had witnessed death. Everyone I knew understood the particular mix of fear and numbness that only repeated and intense physical suffering can inspire.

When I was twelve, my female friends and I were very afraid

of growing up. I remember during an English class we read a
story in which a man, Sam, loved one person but married another. Laurel, whom he didn't marry, was one of those women
who aspired to support herself in the days, about a century ago,
when women did not often have such aspirations. Valeria, whom
he did marry, was not one of those women. Five of my friends
and I took a vote on whether we would rather be Valeria or
Laurel. We took a secret ballot so no one need be self-conscious
about her vote. To the surprise of all of us, we all except one
voted for Laurel, even though, in the story, she loved Sam a lot
and her heart got broken. I think we voted for her because while
Valeria had Sam, Laurel had courage, and we knew that courage
was the basis of everything we longed to be. Lily stood up and
said, "*I* voted for Valeria," and then she walked out the front
door. Lily possessed many good qualities, including exceptional
courage, and it had never done her much good, so she couldn't
conceive of a life in which good qualities were assets.

None of us knew whether the whole world was infused with
violence. Probably, we thought, it was.

My life turned out differently from my friends'. My parents
moved out to California, and I planned to follow after finishing
the school year and a summer job. When I got out to California,
they were already dying. Sometimes they had a driving need to
make good use of their time, teaching me and making money
to leave to me, but other times they needed to see places, not
faraway places we couldn't afford to see anyway, but what tourist
attractions were left, like Disneyland, Waterworld, the Spanish
missions, the Griffith Park Observatory, and Farmers Market.
Other times, we sat in malls, big empty caves in the nicer
areas—with half the stores closed down—or crowded bazaars
in the lower-rent areas. It seems to me that dozens of times I
stood in air-conditioned gift shops examining postcards to send
to Chicago. At one of those gift shops, I remember reading a

postcard saying that the mission we were visiting sat on El
Camino Real—the Royal Highway, although at the time El
Camino Real had been named, *camino* probably meant "road."
That was the path the Spanish *padres* had taken in founding
their series of missions in California before Los Angeles became
a city. So my parents told me I was living in a city on a royal
highway. My parents liked that. They told me to write it down.
When my parents died, I did not have even one friend in Los
Angeles, and I did not try to make any, because I did not have
the courage.

Over the next few years, I did sleep with a few boys, and
sometimes they had friends, but I had none of my own. So Mark,
Lucas, and Jewel were my first friends since I moved to California. At times, I felt overly interested in them. I would sit in
bed and think about remarks they'd made, qualities I'd seen in
them. On Easter I invited them to a picnic with some of Rohn's
relatives. Lucas couldn't come because he was going to services
with some people he knew. Mark and Jewel were surprised I
invited them because they never celebrated holidays except New
Year's, and, if there was someone around to celebrate with,
Thanksgiving. Auntie said Christmas used to be the biggest
holiday of the year, but later it became New Year's, which was
a mildly apocalyptic holiday, and Thanksgiving, because the
fact that there was less and less to be thankful for made one all
the more thankful for what there was.

I hadn't wanted to celebrate Easter with Rohn's relatives,
but Auntie insisted. Whenever I thought about Rohn lately, I
would have to sit down somewhere on the floor. For some reason
a chair wouldn't do. I would sit there for as long as necessary
and concentrate on not crying, and then I'd get up and go about
my business.

Rohn's grandmother, Alma, lived in a very ritzy nursing
home. Her late husband had made a mint winning at Las Vegas

and had died before he had a chance to gamble away all of his winnings. We held the picnic on the grounds of her place. All the other patients had invited their families, as well.

All afternoon, everyone kept saying, "Let's give Alma a pretty egg," and when I finally gave her one, she waved it in the air and said, "Dammit, take me home."

"You *are* home, dear," someone said. A woman got out a guitar and started singing "Row, Row, Row Your Boat," and Jewel said this was the kind of social event that made her feel not just that she didn't want to be there, but that she didn't want to *be*. Mark went inside once and came out with a slight bulge under his jacket, which turned out to be napkins. Even when I was with him and watching for it, I rarely caught the moment when he actually put something under his jacket.

Two of Rohn's nephews were there, talking about how some famous wrestler's techniques were "already a part of the canon," and Rohn's sister and brother-in-law were talking about a friend of theirs who couldn't get hired as a teacher because he didn't have dentures and the school thought he might scare the children. "I can think of a lot of things I can do without, but my teeth aren't one of them," said Rohn's brother-in-law.

"Don't worry," said his wife. "As long as I'm around, you'll never have to go without your teeth." They looked at each other with satisfaction in their eyes.

So what were we all doing there together? It was just that my aunt had fallen in love with Rohn, and Rohn's sister and her husband had fallen in love, and his parents had once been in love, and so on. That's why I was standing there watching Alma wave an Easter egg in my face.

Like a Giant
Game-Show Board

I worked part-time at the law office, but school was the center of my life. Since I wasn't necessarily interested in acquiring a degree, I could take as many or as few classes as I wanted. I was taking a geology and a botany class. Holding minerals and fossils in my hand gave me a thrill. I tried to picture the rocks' histories, and see the world around them change like a film while they endured, changing only slowly. The other class was weird. Studying plants was, for me, like seeing X rays of people I knew and realizing they were nothing but a bunch of bones and blood. It made them seem more complicated than I'd thought, and less complicated at the same time.

But the paper was what I cared most about at school. I don't know what exactly we were looking for by working on that paper. When someone from the "real world," some richtown journalist, came to talk to us, it didn't really matter much. We knew we would never hold jobs like they held. We didn't think we were talented enough on the one hand, and on the other hand we didn't really think they were talented either. We hated these journalists because they condescended to us and because, deep inside, we weren't sure whether we deserved to be condescended to. They would tell us about what would happen if we ever made it in the real world. But what made one world real and another not? We didn't always want to be us, but we never wanted to be them. That's what they didn't understand.

It was starting to become clear to us, if it was not to them, that someday it would be our children and not theirs who would be inheriting the country, if there was a country left to inherit. So we went about writing our stories and when they came, we envied them and also knew that they should envy us, too.

The administrator Bernard suspected of soliciting student prostitutes was named James Goodman. One night, Bernard asked Mark and me to spy on Goodman, to watch a student's apartment he might be visiting later that night. It was really Bernard's story, but I thought it would be fun to stake the place out. Mark agreed. Jewel said we were all three idiots.

The apartment was in a two-story complex shaped like a U and bending around a swimming pool. So though the building was old, I knew the apartments weren't cheap—the state charged a fee for apartments and houses with pools. The buildings were tan stucco with no central buzzer system, and anyone could walk in. In my aunt's day, complexes like that had been common; everything was spread out and lazy. Today, the compact apartment complexes with tiny apartments had security guards, security gates, cameras, and alarms.

Mark and I sat behind some bushes on the perimeter of the courtyard surrounding the pool. There were cracks everywhere, in the concrete that lined the pool, in the tan stucco, in a window on the second floor. We arrived at dusk. The leaves in all the trees and bushes looked fluorescent as the sun's light passed over them. Mark leaned back on his hands, his knees bent in front of himself. To me, this was romantic. In fact, staking out a grungy apartment with your boyfriend was one of the most romantic things I could think of. I thought how the list of things I wouldn't do for Mark grew shorter every day. I leaned my head on his knees and watched the sun fall from the sky.

"Happy?" said Mark. "Sad? Content?"

"Yeah," I said. All of those.

"Those are pepper trees out front," he said softly. He smiled. "I forgot who I was talking to. You know what kind of trees they are. But did you know they used to plant pepper trees all over the area?" He spoke softly, saying that Hollywood was founded in the late 1880s by a Mr. and Mrs. Wilcox. It was supposed to be a Utopian Christian community, sort of like how some people tried to turn a small section of Arizona into a Utopian community about three decades ago. Now Hollywood was anything but Christian, and Arizona had legalized gambling—the Utopian section was like a private dance club for petty criminals.

Spotlights hidden among the dry plants lit up, shining on the cracked stucco walls. The wind was very steady, like a fan on low, and the dry leaves from the plants rustled with slightly different notes. Mark leaned over to kiss one of my breasts through my dress. I hitched up the skirt around my waist while he unbuckled his belt. We had sex furtively and freely, furtively because we might be seen, and freely because we were taking the risk anyway and that made us feel free. We watched him slide in and out of me. Somewhere in the background I heard an alarm crying out. The alarm made me feel pleasantly panicky.

Later that night I took the first watch, because I always stayed up longer than Mark. Mark lay on his side, his mouth hanging open, pieces of grass in his black hair. The wind jiggled the water in the pool, which looked like a big pot of blue Jell-O. I wrapped myself up in a blanket. A few people came and went. Lamps started snapping off. Mostly everybody's curtains were closed. Three boys with long hair, and voices that seemed just to have changed, knocked on a door, but nobody answered and they left. An elderly man returned to his apartment. Something snapped behind me, and I bungled around for a moment before finding my Mace in my purse. I pointed my gun and watched as a coyote peeked out its head. Neither of us moved, and then he scurried away. I'd seen coyotes in the hills, but never in the flats. He was probably desperate for food—possums, stray cats, garbage.

I saw the old man in his apartment, and then the lights switched off. I thought about how if I had a magic amplifier, I could hear all sorts of sounds from those apartments, both pretty sounds and awful ones. I could hear women and men, and women and women, and men and men, falling in love, or breaking up; children sleeping and parents beating the children they often bragged about; people kissing and dying and taking baths.

When it came time to wake Mark for his shift, it was hard because he was smiling in his sleep, which was rare. Often when he slept, the lines that had already begun forming between his brows deepened. I finally woke him when I was too tired to stay awake. His face twisted into a yawn as he sat up.

"So? Did you see anything?"

"An old man and some boys, that's all."

"That's dry," he said. Because of the prolonged drought,

people had started using "dry" to indicate something bad or undesirable.

"Yeah, but I don't really care. I'm just camping out." I lay down in the blanket we'd brought. "Is it hard to fall asleep on the ground?" And then I was out. I dreamed I was still keeping watch and a man swept past the bushes, so close I almost yelled out. He was so nondescript, so different from the photograph Mark and I had, that at first I didn't recognize him as Goodman. And he passed so quickly, as if he were superhuman, that I doubted myself for a moment. He was leaving, not coming. Then I dreamed he passed again. And again. And again. It was the way those moving pictures that once had been the vogue went through the same motion repeatedly. I think I hated those pictures because I imagined that's what kind of ghosts unhappy people became. They spent eternity acting out the same few moments over and over again. Maybe the moments they acted out were near an important turning point in their lives.

Mark never woke me, and when I got up, it was a cool shadowless morning. A lawn mower whirred far away, and the air filled with smells of cut grass, gasoline, and jasmine. In the distance, low clouds in the hills clung weblike to the Hollywood sign. My back felt very stiff.

"Anything happen?" I said.

Mark studied me for too long. "Nothing," he said. The way he said it, sort of like a challenge, I not only knew he was lying, I also knew that he knew I knew. So that's what I said.

"You know I know you're lying."

He turned away irritably, then tapped at the grass with his fingers. "Look, I'm not sure what's right or wrong here, or if it even matters."

"Well, if he's with a student, isn't that wrong? Isn't that a conflict of interest?"

"What does that mean, 'a conflict of interest'?"

"I don't know. You know. It's wrong."

"You act like right and wrong exist like laws of physics or something."

"They do. They're out there. They do exist."

"If you steal a dollar from your parents, is it right to admit it to them? Say you're twelve."

"Well, I can't honestly say I would admit it, but yeah, I think it's right to admit it if they ask."

"Why only if they ask?"

"All right, whether they ask or not. I'm not saying I would admit it, just that it's right."

"What if your parents will punch your eyes out of their sockets if you tell them?"

"Then you shouldn't have stolen it in the first place."

"What are you talking about? You've already stolen it. Look, maybe you don't get an allowance, okay? But it's too late, anyway. You've spent it, it's gone."

"You shouldn't tell them if they're going to beat you. That wouldn't be right."

"But see, it doesn't matter if it's right or wrong. It's irrelevant. You've stolen it, it's gone. You can't tell them. I'm not saying you should never worry about right or wrong. But maybe you stole it because you had to, and now not telling them is what you have to do. There are things that transcend right and wrong." His eyes glazed over for a moment. "If he was with that student last night, and I'm not saying I even saw him, but if he was, he wasn't there because it was right or wrong, he was there because he had to be there."

"But then you can rationalize anything."

Mark picked up the blanket and said, "Take an end," and we started to fold. "What are you going to say to Bernard?" he asked.

"That I didn't see anything. That way I haven't lied."

"Now who's rationalizing?"

We went to my place to sleep a few hours before going to school. It was a Wednesday, and we started working on the paper late because the whole staff, briefly sick of each other, ate dinner separately. When everyone returned, it was after ten. It was almost eleven when we seriously started work. Something nervous, some nervous energy, hung in the air, but we didn't use the energy to work. As usual, Joe asked all kinds of questions about sex, but nobody laughed the way they usually did. Bernard was excited because, though we told him we'd seen nothing, he thought his story was coming along well. He said he had "about a million leads." He'd been in the journalism program for several years and said this was the best story he'd ever had. He thought it was going to change his life, raise him to a new level—a university or a job in journalism.

About three a.m., we still needed to do a great deal to finish up, so we began working furiously. Since many of the students had been here for years, this city room was mainly the arena in which they measured the success or failure of their lives. Sometimes Bernard, Frank, Joe, Jewel, and even Mark, Lucas, and I, felt this was our last chance to do anything with our lives. And when we almost missed deadline some mornings, it intensified the obsession. Sometimes I felt we subconsciously wanted to come close to deadline.

In the morning when we finished on time, we all felt content and at peace with the world. The editors went to the print shop every Thursday afternoon. Before she left, Jewel sat in her office with the door closed, which meant no one was supposed to bother her. But you could see right through the partition window as she kneaded her nose. Last night she'd been both more intense than usual about the paper and more distracted. She hadn't said anything about Teddy, but Mark said they were seeing each other all the time again. After he said that, I thought I felt

Teddy's presence, suffusing Jewel and the air around her. I
pounded for a second on the partition, and the whole thing shook.
For a second I thought it would collapse. Jewel looked up,
surprised, and I opened the door.

"Can I come in?" I said.

"What do you want?"

"I want you to stop kneading your nose," I said.

"Are you okay?"

"Just stop it," I said.

"Why?" she was saying, but I was already leaving.

"I don't know," I mumbled. I think I was just looking for a
small victory—if she could change that minor element of her
behavior, maybe other things would start to change. It was
ridiculous, I'm sure, but I was practical sometimes. I didn't
want to talk for four hours about her and Teddy, I just wanted
to see change.

Mark and I had taken his car to school, but he needed to
attend a class so I took the bus home. I had to stand up because
I was so tired that if I sat down I would pass out. The bus was
full of poor people, old people, women, kids, and pickpockets.
There was not a white face on the bus. It was hot and airless
inside. We passed a junior high school and I saw two girls
fighting, surrounded by a bunch of other children. The girls'
hands and arms were a blur as they scratched at each other's
face and ears. Everyone on the bus watched out the windows.
I remembered kids' fights from when I was younger, remembered
being in those crowds both repelled and drawn by the sight of
my classmates, sometimes my close friends, bruising each other.
Sometimes we broke up the fights right away. Other times it was
as if we suspended ourselves for a few minutes before finally
breaking the fights up; or not breaking them up, waiting for a
winner. Once, another girl and I argued during gym class, and
after school we met to fight. I was nine years old. I thought I

had three choices: I could get beaten up; I could refuse to fight and lose face in front of my classmates; or I could give myself up to the situation and try to beat her. She and I both concentrated entirely on offense, trying to hit each other without worrying about getting hit. I punched at her with the fronts of my fists, not the insides the way the other girls did it. For the first few seconds all I could think was, When is somebody going to break this up? After that, I was under the fight's spell, and all I wanted to do was kill this girl I didn't hate and who didn't hate me. Then my nose was bleeding and the spell was broken. So I lost. And the truth was that while my friends came home with me and took care of me, there was a part of them that was disappointed. Just as I had been disappointed when they'd lost their fights. Because that was already the most important thing for us: who could survive best.

It was not the violence itself, but the way my friends and I watched the fights without breaking them up, and the way, deep inside, we felt disappointed in our beaten friends, that had always seemed to me the harshest part of those fights. On the bus I remember thinking, for no reason, that I could not be sure how far I had come since then.

Jewel threw a party at her Silverlake apartment that Friday for the paper's staff and a few friends of hers. I'd never been to her place before. It was funny to think of these people I spent so much time with as having homes, lives apart from school. Teddy was there, standing in a corner talking to two men, but he ignored the rest of us.

Jewel's apartment was one bedroom with brown carpeting and a kitchen in which the smell of food clung to the walls. I wondered how she could afford more than one room. The street in front was empty. Immediately in back was a junk-filled lot, but beyond that lay an expansive view of the city: a curving line of palms protruding from a hill; a straight line of palms alternating with streetlights along a road; single palms rising isolated, their oldest leaves hanging in clumps around their trunks. Light came from myriad sources: the three square blocks of Scientology buildings; the round Teutonic Records building shaped like stacked discs; billboards that looked from Jewel's window to be the size of playing cards; a car lot; and cars—flashing, speeding, braking. Hollywood looked like a giant TV game-show board.

When it got late, there weren't many people left, fifteen or so. Teddy and his two friends left without speaking to any of us, and then Teddy returned alone. Mark went out for more beer. I'd been drinking too much and felt tired. I needed to lie down. The brown carpet seemed inviting. I lay down, smelled ashy, sweaty smells. A warm, not unpleasant weight descended on my back, and then a man's voice I didn't recognize said "Hey" in my ear.

"Hey," I said.

From what seemed like far away I heard Lucas saying, "Get off her."

"She wants it," said the man, but he got up.

I listened to everyone's voices.

"If the riots get bad this year, I'm moving to the country," Bernard was saying with animation.

Someone else was saying, "I'm a trained concert pianist. I could put my fingers through your skull."

Joe's squeaky voice rose up clearly above the others'. "It seems the longer I go without a woman, the more education I acquire."

I couldn't make sense of any of this. But I knew I didn't want to leave these people ever. As a matter of fact, I didn't even want to leave this floor. I wished Mark would get back. "Come on, *Cupcake*," said Lucas, lifting me up. He was always saving people's lives. He propped me against a wall and we sat on the floor together. I asked him what he thought of skinny neckties, and he said he was a little too traditional for them.

"What would you do if I suddenly shrunk to twelve inches high?" I asked.

He looked thoughtful. "I guess I'd call your mom."

I started to say, "You mean my aunt," but I liked the thought that he might be able to call my mom somehow.

I asked him whether he'd ever been in love and he said he was, every day of his life. He was just humoring me. But I knew he went to church every week, and I thought his answer might have to do with religion, and to tell the truth I didn't feel like talking about it, so I shut up even though I felt like gabbing.

"I'm going to go stand on the balcony for a while. Don't get into trouble, but if you do, just yell."

"What should I yell?"

"For Superman."

He got up and left. I really needed to pee but felt too lazy to move. I leafed through a copy of the campus paper lying on the floor nearby.

"What are you thinking about?" It was Teddy, kneeling down beside me.

"It says here in this filler that Iowa has the highest literacy rate in America."

"That's not true, it's New York. I know because I was in New York once and I saw a lot of people reading." He leaned against the wall next to me.

I pointed to the story. "I just read it."

"No, I've been to Iowa and New York both."

There was a silence. He'd grown a mustache since the last time I'd seen him.

I looked at the paper again. "The new dean of the college is Balinese," I said.

"Little children give you free drugs on the beaches in Bali."

"My parents went there for their honeymoon and they never saw anything like that." That was the only vacation they'd ever taken.

"Maybe they went to the wrong beaches."

He leaned forward, strangely expectant. I showed him a black spot on my hand. "I've got a disease."

He leaned back with satisfaction and spoke loudly. "You have to focus on not getting diseases, and then you don't get them. I myself take care of myself. I don't even drink bottled water, if you can believe that, but I don't worry about it. I found a worm in my water once, but I drank it just like that. And I don't have any skin diseases. You have to focus on health and you'll be healthy."

"I think—" I started, but he interrupted.

"No, no, *no*," he said. I knew he hadn't known what I was about to say because I didn't even know. He moved his eyeballs around a few times as if exercising them. You'd think all this would make me hate him, but I took a certain delight in his obnoxiousness. There was something about utter bad manners that could hold your interest, for a while anyway. After all, it was better than being a chirp.

I threw something else out. "I like plants," I said.

"I can see how a woman without kids would like them," he said. "I'm not trying to set myself up as an expert on plants, don't get me wrong. I've raised some, but as a man, it doesn't interest me." I pictured him as a little boy, saying to other children, "No, no, this is my toy, and so is this one, and this and this," and finally he would be sitting with his collection of toys, alone.

I staggered to my feet. "I have to pee."

"Suit yourself," he said.

Mark returned and I sat on the floor next to him and Jewel. Jewel was talking about how she wanted to be editor-in-chief next semester—the fall term. "If you guys don't vote for me I'll make your lives miserable. I don't know how, but I will." Across the room, Joe was sitting on a couch staring into space with a bewildered expression, his skinny arms and legs splayed out every which way.

I sipped at my beer and asked Mark what he would do if I suddenly turned into a chair, and he said, "I'd take off all my clothes and sit on you." I asked whether he'd ever been in love before, and he said he thought he was once. "I was sixteen, she was twenty-four." He tapped three times on the wall behind him and looked briefly lost. "I'd told her everything about myself, not that I had any big secrets. But it was like she had a piece of my life after I told her these things, and when we broke up and ran into each other sometimes and stopped to talk, she would bring up things I'd told her in impersonal ways."

"That's a very touching story," said Jewel. "I'm touched, broken-hearted. Really I am." Mark laughed.

"Serves you right for falling in love before you met me," I said. I burped.

"What about me?" said Jewel. "Isn't anybody going to ask me whether I was ever in love before?"

Everyone perked up, interested, but then we all tried to seem casual.

"Were you?" said Mark.

"No," she said. She looked at us coolly. We looked back at her coolly. We were sure she'd loved Teddy a lot, and probably still did. And maybe she would continue to love him even if he beat her again. If that happened, Mark, Lucas, Bernard, Joe, or I would have to help her. That's what we were all thinking as we sat there staring coolly at each other.

Long Ago

I looked out of Mark's rear window, saw the huge shadow of a man in the car behind us. We were talking about Jewel's party from a few days earlier, and Mark was saying he would go crazy if he couldn't go to a party at least a few times a year, but he also would go crazy if he had to go to parties all the time. Tonight was Jewel's father's birthday, and we were driving to her parents' house for supper. Jewel was bringing Teddy—we were going to meet them at her parents'.

The man in back honked at us, and Mark motioned him to go around.

"What's his problem?" I said.

Mark leaned over me toward the glove compartment and got out his gun, in case the driver behind us was trying to start a fight. The previous year, there had been more than a hundred road shootings in Los Angeles. I turned around to look at the guy again. "I can't make him out, but he's real big," I said. "He looks sort of superhuman and subhuman at the same time."

Mark eased the car to the right and stopped so the man could go around, but he was looking the other way so we eased out again. We hit several greens in a row and were moving along quickly when a car went through a red just ahead of us, and Mark hit the brakes hard. Our car made a tremendous screech, as did the car back of us. The man behind us drove up alongside and started yelling something, but both his and our windows were closed so I couldn't make out what he was saying. Mark ignored him, but he kept riding alongside yelling.

"Should I open my window?" I said.

"Maybe we should hear what he's saying."

I lowered my window, and so did the man. "What the hell do you think you're doing?" he said. "I almost crashed into you."

"Sorry. Someone went through the red ahead of us," I explained.

"You've been driving like assholes."

"Close the window," snapped Mark.

I raised the window, and he stepped on the accelerator. The man pulled in behind us. In a few blocks, we stopped for a red light, and about three seconds later there was a crash and the whole car shivered once. The car behind us screeched away to the right. We pulled over, our rear window broken. Out in the street, near where we'd been, lay a baseball bat.

"Wow," I said. "He's quite handy with that thing."

Mark ran his hand through his hair, tapped his fingers on the steering wheel. That was his version of counting to ten. He shook his head and handed me his gun to put away. We continued to Jewel's parents.

You could barely see out the rear window, light breaking every which way. Jewel's parents lived in Silverlake, not far from where Jewel lived. We pulled up a hilly street and parked at the curb. The apartment was in one of those newfangled complexes where all the knobless doors slid open and shut, and where you barely had to scrub to clean the bathroom enamel because it was made of special material that practically cleaned itself. Anyway, that's what Jewel had said. I'd never been there. It was five stories high, with probably at least two layers below, for parking. In front, a huge sign moved in the wind: Silverlake Riviera Estates. I loved the way apartments in Los Angeles had cheesy names. I myself lived in the Hobartaire, on Hobart Avenue.

We were a few minutes late, but Jewel hadn't arrived yet. Inside, the apartment was neat, with piles all over. Perhaps they'd cleaned up for us and just put everything into piles. That's what I did sometimes, except I made only one or two big piles. Hank, Jewel's father, lay on a couch and sat up part way to greet us. "Hey, hey, hey, look who's here," he said, then lay back. Mark tapped edgily at a bureau. This didn't seem like an apartment used to visitors. Jewel's mother, Emmy, shook my hand.

"I guess you're Francine," she said.

"Francesca," I said. "Or Francie for short."

"That's nice," she said, and we smiled politely at each other. She turned to Mark. "Did you have trouble finding the place?" They'd met once at Jewel's.

"No, I've lived in Silverlake."

Emmy went to get us drinks from the kitchen. Mark had said Jewel told him her parents had separated twenty-seven times by her count. They were both as tall as Rohn and Annie, and wide without being fat. Hank was wearing a Cubs T-shirt, with a big "C" in the center.

"Oh, are you a Cubs fan?" I said. "I used to live in Chicago."

"What are the Cubs?" he said. His voice was dutifully polite, but he barely glanced at me because he was watching television.

"They're a baseball team from Chicago. You have a Cubs shirt on."

"Oh, hell," he said irritably, but I didn't know whether he was talking to me or the TV.

Emmy, returning with the drinks, said, "A friend of mine got beat up at a baseball game. You know, at that one where two people were killed for rooting for the opposite team."

"Em, where's the channel changer?" said Hank.

Neither Hank nor Emmy held jobs now, though he'd been a nightclub owner and she'd been a singer a long time ago. Now they were suing a movie theater over a chair that broke while Emmy was sitting in it. She fell off and cracked a hip. Hank told us that he was his wife's "litigation manager." The theater was settling for twenty-five thousand, and Hank and Emmy were waiting for the money. Hank reached out suddenly and shook Mark's hand, and when I reached for his hand, he pulled me over and kissed my cheek wetly.

Emmy, who'd been searching for the channel changer, said, "I don't know where it is. I'm sure it's where you left it." To us she said, "Make yourself at home. Have some candy." She went into the kitchen and Hank kept watching TV, grumbling about having to watch the same channel all night if he couldn't find the changer. Emmy yelled to us from the kitchen, "And don't you kids let him make you change the channels for him. He can get up himself if he wants." Mark and I sat on the floor near the coffee table. I peeled open a piece of butterscotch candy from a bowl on the table and leafed through a pile of old magazines. There was a dried, squished bug between two of them, and I studied him for a while. Mark idly shuffled a deck of cards that had been sitting around.

When Emmy returned she exclaimed, "You can sit on the couch. It's clean."

"Oh, I always sit on the floor," I said. "It's my nature." But she seemed so offended that I got up.

"With my knees, hon, if I sat on the floor, I'd never be able to get up again." I liked it when people I hardly knew called me endearments. The apartment smelled faintly of Swiss cheese, and retouched pictures of Jewel and her brothers and sisters hung on one wall. All of them were staring vacantly into the camera.

"Jewel never mentioned she has three brothers," I said. "I thought it was two."

"She had three of them," said Emmy curtly. "One of them has disowned us, though Lord knows it's us who should have disowned him."

In the adjoining dining room, on the table, sat part of a loaf of bread, a bottle of ketchup, an opened box of crackers, and a cereal box. On the wall behind the table hung a couple of matching rock paintings, with turquoise, tan, and white pebbles. "Those are heirlooms from the 1960s," Emmy said. "My grandmother owned them. Ironically, she got them from a grocery store called Jewel. It was a promotion." Emmy must have seen me now eyeing the dining room table. "Do you want some corn flakes, dear?"

"Oh, my God, go get supper, Emmy. They don't want corn flakes."

"Well, how do you know, Hank?" She looked defiantly at him, then at me.

"I'm fine. I mean, if you want to get me corn flakes, I'll be glad to eat them. I love corn flakes. But on the other hand, I wasn't particularly thinking about eating any. It's up to you. I'll eat corn flakes or I won't. Do you want corn flakes, Mark?"

He laughed at me, and I laughed, too.

"Hank, give her room to sit on the couch," said Emmy. "Are you going to leave her standing there all night?"

"Oh, God," said Hank. They started yelling at each other but Hank yelled louder and finally she stopped. Still, he moved his legs and I sat next to his feet. He pushed his feet lightly into my thigh and I moved over, but in a minute his feet were pushed up against me, so I moved over again. He slipped his toes under my thigh but I didn't have any room left to scoot over.

"Am I in your way?" I said.

"No, no, not at all." He moved his legs. The only time he sat up was to drink beer, and when we ate at the table, he spent the last half of dinner leaning back with his eyes closed. Emmy talked to him chattily and every so often he'd say "ungh" or "gwah" or something similar.

Afterward, she helped him to the couch, and Mark and I cleaned off the table. Jewel and Teddy never showed. While we drank coffee, Mark did some card tricks while Emmy oohed and ahhed. Meanwhile she fawned over her husband. Mussing his hair, stroking his back, she seemed really quite content. He went cold and stiff. Mark and I kept meeting each other's eyes, unsure who should make a move to leave and when the move should be made. It always felt strange to meet the parents of someone I cared for, because they were never what I expected. Emmy put the mute on the TV while eyeing Hank, I guess in case he protested. I wondered whether she'd known all along where the remote was. He lay on the couch, seemingly drunk though he hadn't drunk all that much.

"Where's my daughter?" he said suddenly. "It's my birthday."

There was a silence, and yet now that he'd said that, the room seemed less tense. It was what he'd been thinking all night.

Emmy said, "Jewel was always so—"

"Irresponsible, unpredictable, and unreliable," finished Hank.

"In a lot of ways, the hardest to raise was—"

"Jonas," they said simultaneously.

"He's the oldest," she said.

"The oldest," he repeated. And for the first time, I saw how closely attached Hank and Emmy were.

"He's forty-one now. Never married," said Hank. "He's been in love three times, and got his heart broken all three times." He seemed suddenly shy to be talking to strangers, but he continued, as if unable to stop himself. "If you asked Jonas, he'd say he broke two hearts and got his heart broken once. And maybe, by now, he believes that."

"There's a lot of nice girls who would love to marry him."

"But he doesn't go after them."

"What was Jewel like as a child?" I said.

"Oh, a very nice girl, a cute girl," said Hank. He spoke with animation, a different person now from the one who'd been watching TV before. "Cute but hard, inside and out. If you looked at her when she was thirteen, she had hard little breasts like apples, and a hard little butt."

"That's not what she was asking," said Emmy.

"It's what I'm telling." He sat up part way, angry. "Not a one of them listens to me. They'd all be rich. But my kids, if there's a tough road and an easy road to somewhere, they'll take the tough one. Every time I haven't seen one of them for a while,

I start to hope and imagine them a certain way, and then when I see them, they're never what I expect. But I keep hoping and expecting because I'm basically optimistic. Maybe one day one of them will stop being so foolish. I'm an optimist. I tried to make them strong, tried to foster healthy competition between them." At first his voice had been sententious, then thoughtful, but now it was full of eagerness to communicate. He just wanted to tell other people how he felt and he wanted them to understand.

"You tried to make them strong, the same way your father did for you," Emmy said.

He quickly sat up all the way, enraged. "What are you talking about? My father loved me, he loved me. He bought me a bicycle once."

"I didn't say—"

He turned to us. "My father loved me. It's just he was too young. He was sixteen when I was born. We were born on the same day," he added, as if that proved how close they were. He leaned back again. "He was born January 1, 1974, and I was born on the same day in 1990. I was the first child born that year." He said that proudly, then turned bitter. "A car company pledged that they'd give a car to the first child born that year when he turned eighteen, but I never got nothing."

Emmy was quite alert now. "Tell them your most vivid memory from childhood, Hank," she said. "Tell them."

He moved his eyes to make sure we were paying attention. "It happened when I was ten. My father took me for a walk in the arroyo in Pasadena. That was before they started dumping garbage there. We took a long walk. I remember thinking I'd never walked such a long goddamn way. We passed a cave made by trees, and I saw a naked couple in there, but my father kept walking, even though I pointed the couple out. I kept turning around to watch the couple, but they didn't even notice us.

"My father was going somewhere but I didn't know where. Finally we reached a place. It was funny because it was one of the few places in the arroyo where no one in the big houses on the cliffs could see you down there. They didn't have no view. We were more hidden from sight than the naked couple in those trees. And there was a *place* there, in that hidden part of the arroyo. The place was nothing special, just ground like the rest of the ground. But my father stood there looking at that ground. Something had happened there, but I don't know what it was. I never found out, either. I always planned to ask him but I never did. I went back there when I was older to look for the place, but I couldn't find it. I remember looking up when my dad and I left, and there was a house up on the cliff with a whole wall made out of glass. But the point is, it scared me to stand in that secluded place with my own father. I felt close to him, closer than ever, because I knew there was something important about that place, but at the same time I thought he could kill me if he wanted, if he got mad at me. We were so secluded. The thought came to me as a surprise, He could kill me if he wants." He turned to us. "Is that a thought you ever had about your father?"

I shook my head no; Mark didn't respond.

"That was the year 2000. That year. A man walked on Mars, that year. Three ex-presidents died on the same day in May. Everybody at school was talking about it, you know, was it conspiracy or coincidence? But the thing I remember most about that year was the walk with my father, and that secluded spot." He closed his eyes and stopped talking, as if he'd just been turned off. I got the feeling that it was important to him to tell his story every chance he got, but that he probably didn't get many chances.

Emmy brought out a cake, and we sang "Happy Birthday." After that, it seemed right to leave.

"Cumgain," Hank called to us from the couch.

Outside, Jewel was sitting at a table by the pool in a lawn chair. Teddy sat in the chair next to her playing with her hand, which rested in his lap. One of his hands was twitching, as it had been the night I met him. A blue-and-white umbrella rose from the center of the table. Mark and I sat down. None of us said anything. Finally Mark asked Jewel why she hadn't come in.

"I was listening to music." Some men were playing guitars and singing on the other side of the pool.

"Look, we just spent the whole evening celebrating your father's birthday in there because you asked us to come. So you better have a better reason than you were listening to music."

"I'm sorry. I wanted to come in, but when I got to the door, I tried to open it, but I couldn't. I couldn't."

Teddy was gazing importantly into space. He always seemed aware that people might be watching him.

"Is this where you grew up?" I said.

"No." She stared at the rippling pool. "I just lived here a couple of years."

"Listen," said Teddy, and Jewel came to attention. He took her face in his hands. "Your father owned a nightclub once. He owned a house once. Don't be so hard on him."

"He was right here the whole time. And you know how he has those pictures in the back room, where he's posing with famous actors and actresses? Did he show you those?" She whipped around to face Mark and me before turning back to Teddy. "Even then, as the photographer was taking those pictures, he was right here. When he was greeting people in his nightclub, all the time he was right here. This is where he was born, he just doesn't know it."

Mark reached into a pocket and pulled out a handful of butterscotch. He dropped the candy on the table and Jewel picked up a piece and unwrapped it part way. "These always remind me of being a kid." She sniffed the candy and threw it into the pool. We watched it sink to the bottom, the gold wrapper twitching like fish fins.

Teddy started asking me a lot of questions, maybe testing to see what Jewel had or hadn't told me. In fact she'd told me almost nothing since the night we'd bailed him out of jail. "So I guess Jewel told you that I work in real estate?" he said.

"I can't remember."

Jewel listened dispassionately.

"Yeah, I started when she and I lived in Pomona."

I glanced back at her parents' apartment. The lights were off but the television was still on. The courtyard was pretty. It was too dark to see that most of the plants were fake. But I knew by their sound. There were lots of different types of palms, stubby ones and long ones and several in between.

"What story are you working on at school?"

"Fee deadlines. Nothing important." I squirmed. He had a way of leaning forward and talking close to my face that made me uncomfortable. I could feel his breath on my skin. Mark moved forward in his chair and Teddy leaned back.

Teddy said, "Trust is the foundation of the world. It's part of a journalist's job to establish a relationship of trust with the reader. But maybe you know that." He leaned forward again and I leaned back and Mark moved in his chair. "You know what the most trusting thing you can do with another person is? Sleep with them. I don't mean have sex, just sleeping. They could be laughing at you while you're sleeping."

"They could be laughing at *you* while you're sleeping." Mark corrected him, but wouldn't look at him, acknowledging Teddy and ignoring him at the same time.

"I'm just saying," said Teddy. He shrugged at me like, "I tried to help you." He leaned forward yet again. I felt as if his fingers were mashing my brains around, partly to find something out, and partly just for the sport of it. He moved his head sharply and frowned again. "Are you a vegetarian?"

"No."

"Vegetarians don't have enough blood in their veins," he said with disgust.

Jewel asked Mark, "How were my parents?"

"Okay. Your father seemed disappointed that you didn't show up."

"I haven't seen them since last year."

"Vegetarians don't have hungry eyes," said Teddy.

"I guess I should at least make an appearance," Jewel said. She got up and we followed her inside.

Her parents were watching television. Emmy wordlessly got up to get food for Teddy and Jewel. No one said hello to anyone else. Once, Hank sat up, looking suddenly sick, and he glanced, frightened, at Emmy. She got halfway up and they remained in their positions, frozen, until he shook his head and said, "It's nothing." Emmy sat back down. I found that moment touching. They'd both had exactly the same expression on their faces, not a shared love so much as a shared fear.

It started to get late but Jewel gave no sign of stirring. Teddy laughed at the television. Mark took my hand and led me out —we didn't say good-bye and neither did anyone else. The lights of the hills in the distance were muted by fog. Jewel had once said that in her opinion, the last time her parents had had sex was when her twenty-year-old sister was born. But I thought they did have sex, in a slightly ashamed way—ashamed not

because of how much they didn't want each other but because
of how much they did.

Mark stared down the street, at the palms and the cars and
the buildings, and I knew exactly what he was thinking: Long
ago, before any of us was born, none of this had existed. There
had been only fields and hills, and maybe some pepper trees.

Outpost

Every Wednesday night at school we all ate out together, or else a couple of people went to buy food for the others. One night Joe and I got food chores. We drove to a sub shop on Hollywood Boulevard. It was just getting dark. Westbound traffic had stopped because a car—probably an electric one, they were so unreliable—had broken down and they were pushing it off the road. It had been a smoggy day. Even from the boulevard, you couldn't see the Hollywood sign in the hills. On days like this, each neighborhood seemed especially contained, because you couldn't see beyond it. I pulled into a parking space. Someone in the car behind us shook his fist at me, I have no idea why. Many stores, even the ones that were open for business, used wooden boards rather than glass for "windows." Other windows, of unbreakable plastic, were slightly less shiny, slightly less clear, than the glass ones. I was glad to be out. I was spending too much time at school lately.

The sub shop was high-tech clean, with mirrors on several sides and smooth white tables, and lighting that washed the color out of everyone's faces and covered everything—the people, tables, and walls—with a grease-like sheen. There were two men at a table wearing shiny black boots, and wallets on chains around their necks. Tattoos covered all the exposed parts of their bodies, tough tattoos like crossed knives dripping blood; snakes; guns. I was fascinated by tattoos lately, because Mark and I were going later that week to get matching ones, bracelets on our left wrists. Tattooing had been having one of its periodic resurgences for the past couple of years, though that seemed to be waning. As had happened in past centuries, several European royals had gotten prominent tattoos. Now it wasn't uncommon to see people walking down the street with stripes on their faces, or beautiful designs. Those people always made me nervous because I felt they were obliterating themselves, but I knew they would say they were doing the opposite, bringing themselves out for everyone to see more clearly. Mark had a flying crane on one of his arms, and before it had become a tattoo, it had gone through swelling, crusting, and shedding—bits of skin peeling off in translucent colored flakes.

The smell of french fries permeated the air in the sub shop. Something about the lighting made all the noises in the place take on an extra importance. Joe and I stood in line to order. I thought with surprise that I'd never been this close to him before. He had a long profile with an indistinct chin, and his skin was eaten-looking with a new kind of acne people were starting to get. He was staring straight ahead but turned abruptly. "I know," he said. "I'm ugly."

"No," I said. "I wasn't . . ."

"It's okay." He spoke eagerly, not wanting me to be mad. Sometimes passersby would say things like, "Look at the face on that guy," or else they'd simply stop and stare. He would laugh, the way he might if they'd just made an amusing but embarrassing joke. But for all that, when I looked at his face, I couldn't find pain in his expression, just innocence.

He left to find a bathroom, and I sat down to wait for our order. A child, about nine or ten, seemed to be waiting for someone at a table near mine. The men with tattoos were talking. There was something strange about them. Their demeanors were genteel, almost prim, the complete opposite of the way they talked and dressed. One of them said, "She's the kind of girl who gets all fucked up and lets you fuck her, and then afterwards she looks at you lying there next to her and says, 'Fuck! I don't know why I let you fuck me. I don't even like you.' " He spoke in a high, girlish voice as he imitated the girl.

The child smiled nervously at me.

"Aw, that's dry, guy," said the second man. "I hate girls like that." Then they had a conversation I liked, about gardening and the new generation of water-retaining polymers.

"Tubes?" said the girl. She smiled sweetly at me.

"What?"

"Tubes?" She leaned forward and hissed, "Drugs, stupid."

"No, thanks." She yawned and turned away. "How old are you?" I asked.

"Forty-seven. How old are you?" I didn't answer and she said more loudly, "How old are you, Miss Nosy?" Before I could reply she asked again, over and over, shouting, "How old are you? How old are you?" She looked suddenly out of control.

"Stop it," I said sharply, and she did stop, seeming surprised that she might have been doing anything that would bother anyone.

The tattoo men were looking at me. The cashier said to the girl, "Hey, get out of here." Then he ignored us; no doubt we were nothing unusual to him. We all turned to watch a crowd of about a hundred people walking down the street together, hassling people for money and occasionally jostling passersby.

I heard Joe talking to a woman at a table. They were laughing, and she motioned him to sit down, which he did. The woman was wearing a great deal of makeup. She was quite pretty, yet strange in the same what's-wrong-with-this-picture way as the two men. I thought of Hollywood Boulevard as a place that made you all of a sudden crave both darkness and light, and feel satiated with neither by itself. But you couldn't be sure what the right balance was that you craved, so sometimes the balance came out wrong, and you ended up with middle-class white guys in shiny black boots, or right-looking girls who were somehow wrong.

Joe was laughing, really happy, and it was infectious. It really warmed me. The child had changed tables to sit next to a new customer. After I paid for my order, Joe and the woman were still talking in matching twangy voices. Finally the woman got up and left and he walked dazedly over to me. He sat down. The men at the next table looked at him, then at each other, then didn't speak. "Nice girl," said Joe.

"She seems interesting," I said.

"I guess she's okay." He spoke with a slight swagger. He was sort of bragging, just trying it on for size. "She's from Portland. She just moved down here." He caught his reflection in a mirror and rubbed his face doubtfully. "She's going to let me call her." Dazed again. "Do you think she'd like a movie?"

"Sure."

"So we should go to a movie if she wants?"

"Sure. Or make her dinner so you can talk more."

He pondered that. "What if I can't think of anything to talk about? I'll take her to a movie."

We returned to the city room. Joe had told me not to mention the woman to anyone, but within half an hour he'd told everyone he'd "met a girl" at the sub shop.

"He met her," murmured Jewel, "but did she meet him?" But no one said what we were all thinking, that she might be a prostitute.

It was about nine thirty. Matt Burroughs, the student who'd been convicted of murder, stopped by the city room to talk about his case with Mark, Bernard, Jewel, and Lucas, who were all working on his story. Matt was a celebrity among us. Mark didn't like him, but he believed he might be innocent. Matt was average height, with a strange spacy face, bulging eyes and lips. He always seemed confused, but happy to be that way. Though he possessed a boyish face, he was bald except for long curly hair along the hairline above his neck and ears. His hair was blondish with highlights the color of certain root beer candy. Now he wore a beret, and his hair was in two braids as thin as one of my little fingers. He peered at the room over a pair of wire-rimmed glasses.

I was working on a story about parking fees, as usual. Eloise, a new girl Jewel hated, sat across from me. Because her hair was black and bobbed, Jewel called her Lois Lane, and it had stuck. Lois was a chirp gone haywire. She wore dresses with lace and flowers, and fake fingernails that came loose whenever she typed. They didn't fall all the way off, they just hung there, flapping. When she was done typing, she would fix her nails with various glues and polishes. Jewel thought this was a frightening sight and would make Lois go to the bathroom to fix her nails. I guess she bought her nail paraphernalia at a bona-fide drugstore. I hadn't been to a store like that all year. Joe had asked Lois out seven times, but she'd declined.

Matt spoke in a monotone, yet his voice was lovely, soothing. He was telling his story again, from what I could make out. "So then the cops say . . . I didn't . . . I was there, I admit that . . . I was running back and forth watching, in case they needed a witness."

Everyone listened patiently, though they'd heard it all before. Someone offered him a sandwich. There was going to be a rally for him in a couple of weeks while he was still out on bail, and another rally in the fall when his trial started. I couldn't imagine him in jail because he seemed so gentle, and yet I could imagine it, because I thought prisoners would tolerate him. He was an outsider like them and they would intuit that. "They treat you like an animal in jail, so you act like one," he was saying, not at all gently. His lips curled almost imperceptibly. Maybe I was wrong about him. Maybe I couldn't tell who was good or who bad, who was lying and who telling the truth.

Lois was typing furiously, her nails flapping like finger demons trying to escape.

Matt said something and everyone laughed. I wished I could be in there rather than doing a story on parking fees. They were raising the fees ten dollars, which I guess someone had to write about, but I wished it didn't have to be me.

I stopped typing as he walked out of the office. He was slightly pidgeon-toed in the way that certain young boys are. He was thirty-six, but he seemed much younger, maybe not a child but an adolescent, about fifteen. He stopped curiously at Lois's desk. "Typing is a lost art," he said, and we all cooed as if he'd just said something clever.

"I can type a hundred and twenty words a minute," Lois said proudly.

He came around and read my screen, shaking his head. "They keep raising the fees."

"Parking used to be free a long time ago," I said.

He shook his head and smiled his confused, happy smile. "Typing is a lost art," he said again.

"I'm not very good. I'd rather have a dictatyper, but the department can't afford it."

Several people walked downstairs with him, to see him out. He was our journalistic mascot, I guess.

We were putting out only a six-page issue this week, so we finished early. At about three a.m., Mark sat down next to me. He was pale, and the circles under his eyes were so dark he seemed almost bruised. He looked at the clock, but it was jerking back and forth. "It's about three," I said.

"Are you ready?"

"Yeah."

Jewel was threatening Lois, waving a gun around. "I said you are not to do your nails in the city room, do you hear me? Get out of here."

Mark and I started to leave. "Francie?"

I turned. Jewel pulled us aside. "Listen, do you think—are you staying at Mark's tonight?"

"Yeah, why?"

"Do you think I could borrow the keys to your place?"

"What's wrong?"

"Teddy," said Mark to me. To Jewel he said, "If she wants to give you the keys, you have to promise he won't ever know where you were tonight and where she lives."

"I promise."

"Did he hit you?"

"No, no. No. Not really. No, I would say he didn't hit me. I don't think you could say that." She wasn't upset. She just seemed worried that we might be upset, or maybe she was scared that we would take him from her somehow.

"I'm serious," said Mark. "I don't want him knowing where she lives."

"I said I promised, and I meant it."

"He has the keys to your place?"

She nodded.

She seemed eager to please, the way she'd been when she'd wanted me to help bail Teddy out of jail.

I handed her the keys. "You can give them back to me at school tomorrow."

Mark and I walked to his car silently. I poked him in the stomach. "Should I drive or do you want to be the man?"

"You can drive. I fear nothing."

Just because he said that, I screeched into the street, going in the wrong direction to get to his house.

"Say 'Uncle, I surrender, please, please, I am your slob-bering, groveling slave.' "

He repeated what I'd said, and I turned toward his home. Vermont Avenue was empty. Late at night virtually no one, even the chirps, followed the traffic lights. If a light was red, you paused, then went forward if there were no cars coming. Now and then we'd pass a bus stop, mostly at important intersections, where ten or twenty people stood. I didn't know whether they were people who worked late, or people who worked early. I pulled over while three ambulances came up behind me and passed. Maybe there'd been a mini-riot somewhere. Ambulance drivers were trained in using guns and always carried them. I didn't know what I thought of the riots; you got used to them. They'd become so commonplace, I didn't think much about them at all. But a few days ago there'd been a big riot in richtown. That frightened me and thrilled me at the same time. When

richtowns across the country started to fall, I knew there would
be changes. I guess I thought the same as most people, except
in my personalized way—I thought that no matter what happened, people would still need newspapers, they would still
need plants. So I'd have a place in the new order. If the riots
got bad, many people had plans to leave the city. Auntie and
Rohn had always said they would leave, but I hadn't decided
what I would do. I didn't think conflagration was coming; conflagration was destined to fail. Collapse was coming. The city
had been deteriorating for a long time, and it was just that the
rate of deterioration seemed to be increasing.

I opened my window and listened to the plants we passed,
listened for the real ones.

"Do you think Jewel's going to be okay?" I said.

He wrinkled up his forehead, looked down at his beautiful
long hands. "No," he said shortly. "Do you?"

"We can take care of her."

"We can't lock her up."

I stopped at a green light as someone whizzed through. I
hated the ones who didn't even pause to see whether there was
any oncoming traffic.

"Who was the girl Joe met?" said Mark.

"I don't know. I didn't get a real close look at her."

"Was she a prostitute?"

"Maybe, I don't know. He says she's from Portland. I don't
know. If she's a prostitute, why is she going on an actual date
with Joe?"

He shook his head, worried, then glanced in back. "I need
to get that window fixed."

Mark lived not far from downtown. The shops in his neighborhood were lit with dim light, every other streetlamp turned
off. On one corner, we passed the store for *artículos religiosos*,

where he often bought refills of shampoo and soap. They kept things like shampoo, soap, and deodorant among the rosaries and Jesus statues and three walls of candles.

Mark's apartment was in an old brick structure surrounded by stucco buildings. The trees and plants—all real—in front of his place looked wounded, as if the infrequent rain that fell on Los Angeles fell even less frequently there. The neighborhood's newer buildings, some built decades ago with government help, were cream stucco, trimmed in chipped pink, aqua, or deep gold. In the night, they seemed unreal, like things that had died with smiles frozen on their faces.

We circled for a parking space. Down the street a meter maid was writing tickets. Sometimes, if you were unlucky and they hadn't filled their quota, they wrote you a ticket whether or not you were illegally parked. Mark made sure to park in the area she'd already passed, to minimize the chance of getting ticketed for nothing.

The bulb in Mark's foyer was dim, and the stairwell was in darkness except for a tiny light marking each floor. We were going to the fifth.

In his room he flopped down on the bed. His apartment was filled with odd bits that he'd picked up here and there. Often it was cluttered, but tonight it was empty. There was a couch-bed, a table, the bare dull wood floor. The doors we'd gotten near UCLA were long gone, sold to a family down the street. There was someone in the building Mark could have sold them to for more, but Mark didn't like to deal with him. The guy was always insisting you trade things, sometimes even what you were wearing. Once, he stood in front of me and said, "I like your shoes." He would not get out of the way, so finally I took off my shoes and handed them to him. He handed me his jacket and said, "Keep the change." I considered burning the jacket but decided against it.

Sometimes when one of us was in a bad mood, we didn't speak before or after sex. It kept things separate, kept it sex and only sex. Mark was in a bad mood now, a cold mood. Love was new to me. Sometimes I wondered what the limits were of what I would do for someone I loved. Afterward, he stared toward the ceiling and didn't talk. It wasn't a warm tired-after-sex silence, but a cool silence, a chilling one. I gave him the right to those silences because I loved him.

We hadn't said anything about this coolness tonight, but before he closed his eyes he said, "I'm sorry. I love you." I didn't answer and he closed his eyes. I never answered when he said he loved me, just lay in silence. He gave me the right to those silences. I felt that if you said something out loud it could be taken away.

Mark fell asleep. I thought I could hear the sound of static from the TV above us. Sometimes we heard the "Star-Spangled Banner," and then a couple of hours later, programming would resume. I didn't think the TV was ever turned off.

I felt very at-home in Mark's place. I thought of his apartment as a safe spot. It was like in Chicago when a friend of mine used to live over a former boathouse. Sometimes when I slept over at her house, we went down there and met some of the other kids, staying till morning. The boathouse was full of disintegrating wood, dried seaweed, and mold that grew in fabulous flowerlike shapes. A couple of times Lake Michigan was covered with dead alewives. The smell was overpowering, but the fish themselves were lovely, the way they looked like silver cobblestones on the lake. We felt we could walk out there on them. If I had a crush on a boy, it seemed very romantic to shiver next to him, a radio pressed to our ears between us. In the morning someone would go to a bakery for fresh bread. I was really happy out there in that boathouse, eating bread in the middle of that sort of flowering desuetude. We belonged there, in a place that wasn't even meant to *be* a place any longer. It was impossible for us not to feel special and brave there. It never occurred to me that any of us—or any of the other kids in my class—would one day become what some of us became: a girl who daydreamed ten hours a day and couldn't hold a job; a girl who had four abortions in high school; a nurse with a drug problem; a lawyer who chased ambulances, and later tried to kill himself. Lying there, kissing the boy next to me, or sleeping, dreaming that the boathouse was a houseboat, I was vulnerable and invincible at the same time.

I got up, went to Mark's window and opened it, sitting naked on the sill and feeling the rush of cool air against my skin. Everything was desolate now, but the area bustled during the day and on weekend nights. In the afternoons there would be clusters of unemployed men drinking, and teen-aged boys and girls flirting. There weren't that many unsupervised children around, even during the day, except going to and coming from school. Beyond the wide, mostly flat landscape of the neighborhood rose downtown Los Angeles. Now fog broke off the tops of the buildings, the logos smiling through like colored moons. Because the skyscrapers were surrounded by relative flatness, they did not seem so triumphant as those in the Chicago skyline had. They seemed, as I saw them from Mark's window, more like an outpost of some sort.

This community wasn't affluent enough to support a supermarket, so there were only a few *grocerías* and *carnicerías* where the goods were overpriced. In the afternoons you could buy produce at one of the trucks that often parked out on the street, usually selling vegetables, occasionally selling nothing but melons and apples.

Goose bumps rose on my arms, just slightly, but I liked the coolness. I could see a large, one-story building that was an abandoned supermarket on Pico Boulevard. They were talking about turning it into a church. In front of the supermarket a truck parked every afternoon to purchase metal, glass, and paper by the pound. When I was little, my friends and I used to collect bits of broken glass and sell it to recyclers for a few nickels, which we gave to a classmate who was planning to run away from home.

On a corner a few feet from where the recycling truck parked, men and women with faces and hands of leather sold pillows, cushions, and rugs. Often I saw children napping in the dirt next to the pillows, sitting on a nearby bus bench eating breakfast, lunch, or supper with their mothers, or sleeping among the bags of cans in the truck. I ached with the thought that the odds were worse for them than they had been for my school friends, that one day when they were older many of them would wake up in the middle of the night with the certain knowledge that the world was too hard for them; and yet the next morning they would get up again and go about as usual.

Tattoo City

Auntie Annie told me that her mother used to take her shopping, which was supposedly a fun, female thing to do. She talked wistfully of going to a big department store in the morning and not emerging till dark. She and her mother tried on clothes and jewelry they couldn't afford. Once in a while, they'd splurge. I wanted to do something for Auntie, but I couldn't really take her shopping, even if we had been able to afford it. There weren't that many department stores left, for one thing. There were a few big bazaar-type malls, but Annie could sew better than the people who made clothes for most of those places. She could sew better than the people who made expensive clothes, too, but she tried to explain to me how it was fun to buy from department stores just for the sake of buying from them.

My job at the lawyer's provided me with a way to take her "shopping." Most of the cases the lawyer I worked for handled were bankruptcies. One of his clients was a family who'd taken out loans using the homes they owned as collateral. They'd made small down payments on the homes, and when they got all the loan money, they left the country. They were personal friends of my boss, and he asked me to go to their places and clean up, taking anything I wanted they'd left behind. I took my aunt to one of the houses, the nicest one, where I planned to empty the pool and clean up.

The house was in a camp—one of those communities enclosed by tall metal fences and guarded by uniformed, armed men and women. Camps had become more and more popular over the years, not just for the wealthy but for everyone. This place, called Steeplechase Farms, had houses ranging from stately to extravagant. The house I was supposed to clean out was trilevel, with an acre of sloping land behind the back yard and the pool. I placed one end of a garden hose into the pool and the other end down a hill until the water slowly started to drain. The family had left only a couple of months ago, but much of the water was already brown-green and sludgy.

Auntie hadn't lost any weight, yet when she stood on the diving board gazing at the sludgy water, she seemed more like a balloon than a thing of substance. She seemed like something so light that if the wind blew even once it would blow her off the diving board. And she seemed lost and young.

But she got excited when we started going through the house, throwing out trash, keeping what we wanted. It was exactly what I imagined a wild shopping spree was like. We loaded the truck with a chest, a king-sized mattress, two wall mirrors, pots and pans, plant fertilizer, packaged detergent, and clothes. Some of the stuff we took was already packed, perhaps because the family had left in a hurry. I felt as if I were buying Auntie time. She'd worked all her life, and by getting these goods for free, she wouldn't have to spend time working for them.

Once, I found her engrossed in a book or something, and when I peeked over her shoulder she was reading the diary of a schoolgirl in love. The diary was complete with pink heart drawings and exclamations about not being able to go on. How romantic to think that there were people you couldn't live without! The reality was that you could live without them, as Auntie Annie was living without Rohn.

Surprisingly, the electricity hadn't been turned off, but there was only one light bulb in the whole house. I cleaned while Auntie read diaries. We took the bulb from room to room. We'd arrived in the morning and left around midnight—more than twelve hours. It was the most fun I'd seen my aunt have since Rohn disappeared. For a moment, as we were driving on the Orange Freeway on the way home, it was like it used to be, the windows open, Auntie wrapped up in a blanket, the truck full of goods. But she seemed to have had the same thought, and then—I could tell—sadness enveloped her. I decided at that moment that when Rohn had been missing for exactly one year and we could be sure he wasn't going to be released, I would go searching for him again. I didn't say anything to Auntie, but I made the promise to myself.

That Friday, Mark and I went to get our tattoos. Tattoo City was a narrow place crammed in between a McDonald's and a lingerie store. House of Burgers used to be a lot like McDonald's, but they'd developed in different directions. McDonald's had stayed low priced and fast but had stopped serving real burgers, and House of Burgers had become a sit-down restaurant that retained their few real meat dishes.

Mark's tattooist friend, Carl, was well known among aficionados of tattoos. There were several people inside perusing samples on the walls—all manner of skeletons, hawks, and eagles. When Carl, who was about fifty, called us, everyone in the shop looked at him curiously and admiringly. In back was a small spare room, maybe a former kitchen, with a metal sink, a desk, a telephone, a cabinet of colored bottles, and several shelves of nature and art books. The art was mostly ancient Asian, American neographic from fifty years ago, and ancient Egyptian. In another room, a dog barked and classical music played. I felt very nervous to be getting a tattoo. I picked up a book on Egyptian art and riffled through it, barely seeing. I looked at my wrist, at the pictures, at my wrist. I'd never realized how thin my wrist was. "Those Egyptians sure had a way with coffins!" I said, in a tweety voice.

Carl was a tall, bearded man, arms covered with tattoos. There was something both kind and hard about him, both intellectual and feral. He held out his arms for us and we looked them over as if examining goods in the case of a jewelry shop. "This is nice," I said. "And this." Carl beamed.

"Do you ever tattoo yourself?"

"Sure," he said, a bit tiredly.

"Do you get asked that all the time?"

He nodded. "We're never original in new situations, are we?"

Mark and I leafed through the books, looking for colors and designs we liked. He asked me to choose because he was color-blind. I wanted to make sure to choose colors he would like if he saw them as others did. Mark was telling Carl we both might transfer to a university at some point.

"Well, aren't you fancy," said Carl. "Aren't you two fancy. Congratulations." Actually, Mark had told me, Carl held a Ph.D. in art history. He beamed again, happy for us.

After I chose what I wanted—a flowered vine from an ancient Japanese panel—Carl went into another room to make the tracings and transfers. His golden retriever alternately glared at us and scratched behind his ears. "Can we maybe have red instead of the blue in the picture?" I called out.

"If you want, but red will fade. In about ten years all you'll have left are the outlines and the other colors."

Ten years! "Wow, I'll be in my late twenties."

"By the way, did you want me to go first or do you want to?" said Mark.

"It depends if it hurts."

"Of course it hurts!" Carl said sharply. He leaned into the doorway and added soothingly, "But it's not ego-wrenching pain, darling, it's way down there on your wrist, and it doesn't have anything to do with your soul at all."

"Don't think of it as sharpness touching you," said Mark. "Think of it as something real cold or real hot. Maybe that'll help. Pretend you're being touched with coldness or heat, not with sharpness."

"Once it starts getting numb it hurts less," said Carl. "The body has ways of protecting itself against pain."

"You guys aren't helping much. I mean, I'm going to do this, but you aren't helping." Carl put out his palms like, Tell me how to help you and I will. "So how did you get started in this business?" I asked. Carl returned to work without answering. "Is that another standard question? That's okay, because I don't mind sounding . . ."

"Stupid. You don't mind sounding stupid?" he said. Mark rubbed my back, letting me know that Carl didn't mean anything, it was just the way he was.

"He was in advertising art," Mark said, "but he lived near a tattooist."

"What if after I get this tattoo I see other designs all the time and think I should have done something else instead?"

"That's why God gave you so much skin," said Carl. He poked his head out once more. "Does she know when I'm kidding?"

"No," said Mark.

"Neither do I," he said. "But this is on the level. We each have the responsibility to interpret God in our own way. He might be up there making all sorts of important decisions, but what does that have to do with you or me? We still have to decide, Do I want this for a tattoo, or that?"

Carl returned to the room, his hair falling onto his forehead. He had a look in his eyes as if he'd just drunk eighteen cups of coffee, but it wasn't that he was out of control, it was just that he loved tattooing. That was the look, very revved up. I got up on a tall padded bench, rolled up my sleeve, and stuck out my arm. He stared at both sides of my wrists without speaking for a full minute. "The ideal tattoo is the one that turned the jackass into the zebra," he finally said. "That's what we want to do here, turn your wrist into something it was meant to be."

I pulled my arm back. "Wait, this is like getting married or something. Let me think a minute." Carl took off the pair of gloves he'd put on and got out a cigarette. He dropped his lighter, and when he leaned over to retrieve it, I saw the crack of his ass, and the top of a huge tattoo on his left cheek. He got up and turned abruptly.

"Don't let the thought that it'll hurt change your mind. It's not enough pain to make you alter your decision! I'm not going to lie and say it doesn't hurt, but if you want a tattoo, it's worth it!" He spoke passionately, as one with a fervent belief in tattoos.

"I want to have one, I just don't want to get one." I put out my arm again and he asked me to lie down, which I did. He cleaned me off and applied the transfer. Lamps, bottles, and utensils were partially covered with cellophane, and once Carl had put on gloves, he touched things only on the covered parts. He was using a small, old machine he said he hadn't used in weeks. He told us he never used a tattoo machine on two customers in a row, and he used only disposable needles. His ex-wife, who lived in San Francisco, made his tattoo machines for him. "She's the best in the business," he said.

Mark took my right hand. It reminded me of the way a nurse had pressed my uninjured arm in the hospital when I'd been hurt. And it had the same effect, giving me a visceral feeling of comfort. There's something hypnotic about someone's touch when you're hurting. When Carl started, I tried to imagine it was ice on my skin, as Mark had suggested, but it hurt too much for ice. I trusted Carl. I guess you had to trust someone to let him draw on you with a needle. It seemed weird to think that all those people out there with tattoos had trusted someone, a lot, when they didn't even know him. Carl's touch was firm and steady. He rubbed me over and over with cleaning solvent as he worked. Cold air from a window blew lightly on my face. "Almost done," said Mark.

"Ahnn," I said.

"What are you laughing about?" said Carl.

"I'm whimpering."

"My clients do *not* whimper."

His face was tense, concentrated, lost in the lines on my wrist. When he finished, I looked at the colors and thin lines. They were mixed with blood and swollen, so they seemed more like a colored scar than colored skin. As Carl lit a cigarette, he studied the tattoo from the corner of his eyes. His eyes were gleaming, and I knew he was very proud. Both of us were drained. Even Mark seemed tired. Carl bandaged me up and

got us coffee. "Let's take a break." He talked about some of
the places he'd lived—New York, Chicago, and Philadelphia
—and it seemed he thought everywhere he'd lived and everywhere he might live was better than Los Angeles. I knew how
he felt. Auntie, Rohn, and I had always dreamed about getting
away from the smog and the riots, but for some reason we stayed.

Carl was moving soon to a small desert town a few hours
away. He said there were two essential types of place names in
Southern California that held beauty. There were the ones with
Hispanic roots, like Los Angeles, San Diego, Mira Loma, and
Santa Ana. And there were the ones for the desert towns, like
Twentynine Palms, Thousand Palms, Yucca Valley, and Joshua
Tree. He was moving with his shop. As he talked, I felt tension
drain out of me. I felt as if I were a child and he a grownup
telling fairy tales. The dull pain from my wrist was an incredible
relief from the sharper pain of tattooing. Mark took off his watch
to get ready for being tattooed. An hour had elapsed while Carl
was working on me. I felt very emotional. It was something about
the permanence of the blue ring around my wrist, something
about the pain, something about the plainness of the shop and
Carl's pride in his work. "There's a lot of tattooing going on in
places where it's illegal," he was saying. "There's just starting
to be a reaction against all the tattooing that's been going on.
New York City just outlawed face tattoos."

I jumped up suddenly and flung my arms around his neck.
"Thank you, thank you, thank you!" I said. "It's over, I'm free,
and I have a tattoo."

We all laughed. He took out a different machine to work
on Mark, but Mark said he wanted him to use the same one.
As the machine buzzed, I held Mark's free hand. When the
needle first touched him, he winced almost imperceptibly. I
thought it must be strange to be a man and not be allowed to
say, "I hurt." I kissed his fingers.

"We're not in competition at all." Carl was talking about another shop. "I'm a daytime shop, they're an evening one. We do different types of work." Then he had to stop talking for a while to concentrate.

When he finished, we all felt very proud, Carl because he'd done the work, and Mark and I because that was part of the whole point of getting a tattoo. It was almost as if you were challenging God. That thought gave me a chill and I knocked on wood.

Mark and I were supposed to meet Jewel for a drink, so Carl closed up shop to come with us. Jewel was already at the bar, sitting by the doorway, but she didn't acknowledge us when we came in. "Are you okay?" said Mark. But she just started pushing distractedly at her nose.

"What happened?" Mark said, but she shook her head no.

She made us feel depressed so nobody wanted a drink anymore. Mark decided we should drive up into the hills, so we got in the car. On Hollywood Boulevard, there were a lot of boys with long braided hair, and teen-aged girls with designs painted on their faces. There was a crowded bus in front of us, and a crowded bus behind us. About twenty or thirty people waited at each bus stop. We passed a small crowd around a man holding on to an infant. The man was waving for a police car, and the baby seemed hurt. The bus back of us honked and Mark stepped on the accelerator. I turned to watch, the infant's face blank, the man's face wild. The police car pulled over. The man's mouth was open but no sound was coming out as we drove away.

Mark took us up to the observatory, one of my favorite places. There were a bunch of motorcycles in the parking lot. I watched Carl eyeing someone's tattoo. His art was probably walking all over the city.

It was early evening, still light out, and unusually humid.

My bandage was getting damp with perspiration. We went down to a private place Mark knew, and looked out at the city. All at once, streetlights shimmered on. I thought that was good luck. Jewel sat down where we'd led her. She was like a rag doll. I think if we'd set her down in the middle of a crosswalk downtown she would have limply complied.

Carl grew increasingly agitated as he watched her. "Here's how I see the meaning of life as it relates to tattoos—life hurts more. I can't wait to get to the desert." I imagined him driving down I-10, by the dinosaurs erected near a diner on the side of the highway, by the fields of windmills and solar panels, by miles and miles of Joshua trees. Finally, in the middle of all that heat and dryness, he would set up Tattoo City. I pictured the shop's sign out there in the desert.

"Did somebody hurt you, too?" I said.

"Not like you're thinking. Not anybody special. Not all at once."

Jewel began sobbing. "There's somebody else," she said between sobs. "He has another girlfriend."

Nobody spoke while that sank in. Mark was disgusted. "You're crying because he's beating up someone else instead of you?"

The moon was a white sliver in the gray sky, hovering near a silver comet that looked like a star moving slowly. When I was a child my mother always used to say, "Why can't the earth be more like the moon?" She didn't mean like the moon as it would be if you were on it—dry and airless—but rather the peaceful, lucid moon you see from earth. She used to ask me that question whenever I was sulking over something. She asked it in an almost jesting way. It was just a little thing meant to cheer me up. And sometimes it worked, too. Just the thought of the beautiful moon in the sky made me feel better. My parents used to own a delivery business like Auntie and Rohn's. During long drives we often got out to stretch late at night. I remember that if it was cool out, I liked to sit on the car hood and feel the heat seep into the backs of my legs. Sitting out there was another time, besides when I was sulking, that my mother asked that question about the moon. Then, she would say it like an incantation, as if she were casting a spell around me, to protect me.

Now I remembered my Chicago friend Lily—whose father used to beat her mother—and how both her parents had been beaten as children. Probably so had *their* parents. Probably so had Jewel's parents. You could trace the evolution of violence in their families like you traced the evolution of a species, a sort of family tree of violence. I thought Lily's mother was one of the bravest people I'd ever known, because she's the one who broke this line of violence by leaving Lily's father and by teaching Lily that none of this need ever happen to her.

I didn't know what kind of world this was, where a violent man's infidelity might hurt a woman more than his beatings. I watched the rainbow of smog rise above the city with sunset, then darken and disappear. Jewel hadn't moved for a long time.

"Is she okay?" said Carl softly.

But there was nothing we could do to make her okay. We would have to be able to change her past, and her parents' past, and so on. For now, the best we could do was to stand there.

I think the worst night of Lily's life, at least when I knew her, was the last time her father beat up her mother before she left him. We sat in the kitchen after that beating, feeling the air drift in from the window over the alley, terrified because we weren't sure whether Lily's father was going to hit her mother again. I thought that Lily loved her mother with such force that it was her mother's fear and not her own she felt so distinctly —an animalistic fear, as if at the slightest touch she would jump higher or run faster than ever before. I think that was the night, when I was almost eleven, when I first became a grownup, when I first knew I could take care of myself. I sat there in the kitchen with a glass pitcher in my hand, knowing that if necessary I could crack it on someone's head.

Carl and Mark were making eye signals at me, to go talk to Jewel. I guess it was because we were both women. I sat down next to her, thinking of the night with Lily's mother, of how I knew I could take care of things from then on. But the only thing I wanted to do now was grab Jewel by the arm and shake her, which I didn't do. "It's a weird kind of love," I said to her. "Sometimes when you're with him, you seem almost bored."

"I don't love him when I'm with him," she blurted out, then seemed surprised, the way a puppy is surprised the first time it barks. After a long silence she changed the subject. "I never asked you what you thought of my parents."

"They were nice," I said.

"My parents are a lot of things, but nice isn't one of them."

There was an awkward pause, and then we both giggled.

"Did your father ever tell you that story about the arroyo?" I said.

"He tells that story to everyone. I've always thought I would go to Pasadena one day and check it out personally."

"I'll go with you."

"Really? I'm afraid I'll go to all the trouble, and it'll be nothing. Knowing my dad, he probably just made it up."

"Is he a storyteller? Rohn was like that sometimes."

"Not a storyteller. But he likes to remember things the way he likes to remember things. It doesn't matter if it happened that way or not."

"I believed him."

"I suppose I do too. All right, let's go someday." She coughed a few times. "I've had a cold for a long time. Or maybe it's the pollution getting to me. I hate this rotten town." But the lights of the city lay invitingly before us. She pointed toward Vermont Avenue. "Teddy lives that way. In fact, I think I can see his building." She sat up straighter. "Can you see it?"

"Don't even think about him." She coughed again, turned suddenly, and threw up.

Somewhere toward the parking lot there were yelling and alarms. "Is she okay?" Mark called. "We'd better get out of here."

"Time's up for feeling sorry for her," Carl said firmly. "Get up, Jewel. Come on, Francie. Time's up. You only get five minutes a day to feel sorry for yourself. That's my personal rule."

No One Would Notice

Since I'd had boring assignments all year, toward the end of the semester Jewel assigned me a human interest piece on Matt Burroughs' mother, Madeline. Besides Matt, she had another son, Pyle, who was thirty-four. Pyle used to growl at me. That was one of the strange things. Another was the holes in the roof over The Bead Shop, the store Madeline owned. When I was little my mother used to tell me that holes in a roof were where ghosts came in and out. So I knew that if there were no ghosts in that shop, then there was no such thing as ghosts. But I'm getting ahead of myself.

The first time I'd visited the shop was on one of

those days after a rain when Los Angeles is at its best, the clouds lifting and leaving the sky a clean blue you rarely saw anymore. What clouds remained after the storm were huge and white. It made me feel wistful. I wanted clouds just like that, white and running and lovely, in my heart.

I called Madeline from the law office where I worked and made an appointment for an interview. I told her I'd stop by on a Friday but came a day early, because I was searching for gold glitter and thought she might have some. The lawyer I worked for kept a bag of dirt in the office that he claimed came from a gold mine in Northern California, and he was looking for investors. He would show potential investors dirt to "prove" he owned a gold mine, which, he told me, he really did. So one of the other assistants in the office wanted to put some gold glitter in the bag as a practical joke.

Madeline's place didn't have glitter or trimmings. It was devoted purely to beads. It wasn't like one of those shops full of cheap plastic beads with a few standard wood and glass ones. There were walls and jars and drawers full of every type of bead. There were blue deco beads, painted driftwood, wooden beads of myriad shapes and sizes, antique Austrian glass beads, thousand-year-old Persian beads. In the drawers, Madeline showed me just a few things: theatrical jewelry; amber, which she felt was good for your blood when you wore it; coral she'd found on beaches; and every type of shell—beads so beautiful I knew for sure there were ghosts in that shop.

After she showed me around, Madeline went to work tapping numbers into a calculator. She had the most wrinkly face I'd ever seen. Her skin looked like aluminum foil that had been crumpled into a ball and reopened. I'd just picked up a string of beads and set it down again when Madeline whacked my hand with her calculator. "Don't put it down that way," she said. I hadn't even known she was behind me. She went back to her table. As I listened to the tapping of her fingers on the calculator keys, I became aware of another sound, a growl from a corner. And there I saw her son for the first time. "Don't mind him, that's my boy." He was snarling at me. I stared transfixed. What transfixed me was this: he hated me, you could see it in his eyes. He was wearing a red knit shirt with two embroidered golf clubs over the chest pocket, and a pair of pleated black slacks.

"He looks like Canny Valencia," I said. Valencia was a famous golfer.

"That's what everyone says. Now, Pyle, stop that," she said mildly. He sniffed at the air, then lit a cigarette while keeping his eyes on me. But he stopped growling.

Madeline was standing again. "Where's that necklace that was on the table?"

"I didn't see anything."

She hurried over, and the growling started again from the corner. "Oh, here it is." The growling subsided. "So you wanted to ask me some questions?" She seemed suspicious of me and trusting at the same time.

"Well, can you tell me what Matt was like when he was a boy?" She went back to her calculating and I examined a counter covered with about fifty jars of wooden beads. When she didn't say anything, I turned around to find her staring into space. I bet she could see Matt, as a boy, at that moment. But that wasn't it at all.

"I hate human beings," she said. "I love my sons, but I hate human beings."

"I'm a human being."

"But you're trying to help my son." She had a slight accent, I wasn't sure what kind, and there was something elegant about her, not a learned or acquired elegance, not the elegance of someone wealthy, but the natural animal elegance of someone born both poor and gracious. "What was he like as a boy? He was a different little person every day. Every day, he changed. Every day, he was taller, a better person, a worse person. Different."

I fingered some beads.

"Cedar," she said. "If you oil them they shine."

I bought three cedar beads and left, telling her I would return next week. That night in front of the TV I oiled my beads with cooking oil, and they really did shine after I was finished. To me, beads were like fossils, something priceless and timeless.

I had a new apartment, even smaller than the last but with fewer bugs. The only window looked out toward the airport, and I got up to watch the lines of flashing jet lights beyond the palm trees. The sky was rarely black in Los Angeles, but tonight it was. The rain had cleared the haze.

My apartment was probably exactly the same as a million other apartments in Los Angeles. When you were looking for a place, you didn't have to look that much, because it was all the same apartment if you didn't have a lot of money. The outside of the building was a pale stucco with a brightly colored trim and with fake banana plants and fake red canna lilies lining the front around the entrance. Everywhere you went in L.A., you saw real or phony banana plants, birds of paradise, canna lilies, and palms. Outside my apartment there was a sign saying "The Palms at Franklin, Singles and One-Bedrooms, Vacancy." Inside, my small rectangular room had gold-striped wallpaper and a floor of low-grade foamite. Many of the people in the building were on month-by-month leases, and there were one hundred and fifty units, so all the time people were moving in and out.

I stayed up late, feeling antsy in my apartment. The couple next door moved out at three in the morning. I heard them carrying their things in and out. "Shh, they'll hear us," the girl said at one point, and I wondered who "they" were. Rohn always said "they" was who any one of us would be when in a group.

But it was hard to take him seriously when he said that because at the time he was driving home backward from the grocery store, to upset Annie. I smiled as I remembered how red her face had gotten, yet at the same time she was pleased because he was showing off for her as well as trying to upset her. Life was much grimmer without Rohn around. He was everything that was the opposite of grim.

I bought glitter on my way to work the next day, and the other assistant and I poured it into my boss's bag. We peeked in while he got ready to show his dirt to some clients who were coming by in an hour. I felt bad later because when he first peeked in, his eyes lit up, as if for a moment he believed that some of his dirt had metamorphosed into real gold. Maybe there was something greedy about the way his face lit up, but I thought it was a good thing that he believed such occurrences were possible.

He got so mad he made the other assistant and me remove every bit of glitter from the dirt before his clients arrived. Then he sent me downtown to get some papers stamped at the court-house. I took the bus, since I rarely drove to work, and since I never drove downtown. The biggest parking lot in the world was in downtown Los Angeles, and I liked to avoid going there if I could. It was a horrible concrete dungeon eight blocks long and eight levels deep.

There were people in the courthouse who stamped papers for a living. I guess they did other things too, but that's all I ever saw them do. You handed them papers—in my case, bank-ruptcy papers—and they stamped them and gave you two copies to stamp yourself. They assigned you a court date and you gave them money, and maybe a cred or two if you'd needed some extra attention. If you did anything wrong, they scolded you. They were people with no power at all in government, yet as you stood there waiting in line, you felt they possessed all the power that existed in the world. When I got back to the office, I practiced stamping. I took a hand stamp and stamped pieces of paper over and over. I felt quite violent whomping that paper.

When my boss came in and saw my desk covered with sheets of stamped paper, he licked his top teeth once, twice, three times, and then he said, "Okay, okay. That's okay." He left muttering something about women. He was in a bad state of mind regarding women because his wife had recently left him. He said he sort of understood why she'd left, and he sort of understood why she'd taken the car and the television. But why had she taken the automatic garage door opener? She would never need it again. "Why?" he'd asked me. "You're a woman. Tell me why she did that."

"Maybe she was feeling vindictive," I'd ventured, but he didn't get it. He could understand anger, but he couldn't understand malice.

I went back to The Bead Shop after work to buy nylon to string my cedar with. Madeline told me she used only real fishing nylon that old-fashioned fishermen used. I don't know why it made a difference what kind of nylon you used, but I liked how particular she was. Being particular was like a type of integrity. She talked to me while she counted beads for inventory. She wouldn't tell me where she was from, saying she was a Californian now. But she did say that when she was a girl her family had lived by a buried castle and someone used to pay her and her siblings to search the remains. She didn't know who it was that paid them, just a man who came around. They would get the equivalent of about a penny for every bead they found. Later, she'd been to museums all over the world, studying jewelry and costumes. She'd opened her shop during the twenties after her only divorce—she'd also been widowed twice. Her shop was like a fossil, staying the same, as the rest of the country moved deeper into what newspapers and historians were already calling the Dark Century. "Now the shop's on a steady course," she said, "not thriving and not dying." She designed jewelry for movies sometimes, and lent out pieces for advertisements, but what she liked best was to make necklaces for herself that no one ever saw. They were just for her own personal enjoyment. Usually, she never even tried them on. "I know they'd be beautiful on, but *I'm* not beautiful anymore."

Madeline gave me a blue-and-white bead that she said was one of the beads that white people had used to "buy" the island of Manhattan. "If I ever get to New York, I'll bring this with me," I said. "I'll buy an apartment with it."

"I doubt that," she said dryly.

I looked around. "Where do you get all your stuff?" She winced at the word "stuff."

"I have connections," she said testily. "I'm a bead professional, dear."

Pyle was growling happily to himself in a corner as he played with some brass medallions. Madeline leaned forward, frowning, and whispered, "He's losing his hair, like Matt."

I suppose I ought to have asked her some questions about Matt. That way I could finish my story right away, and maybe they'd put it on the front page while everybody was still interested. But I wandered into another room and looked at the strings of beads on the walls—three walls of beads that she'd already counted for her inventory. She was going to retire soon. She'd chosen all these beads personally for her shop, and now she was going to sell them. They were arranged by color, brown ones, blue, red, yellow. Is this what happened to you in life? You neared retirement and you counted everything you'd acquired, and then you went home for good?

Madeline's shop stayed open till eight most nights. She didn't have many customers, but she liked to work late. Because she was retiring soon, she needed to work on inventory all the time.

I took to hanging around for an hour or two in my spare time. Matt came by sometimes. He possessed a sort of daffy but exquisite confidence in himself that I admired. Pyle was normal looking, while Matt was weird looking, but there was something that drew people to him. He wasn't ostentatiously sincere like bad liars, but there was a simple sincerity about him. Even Jewel said that he was so sweet he drew out her maternal instincts. "You mean you want to take care of him?" I'd asked. "No," she answered. "I want him to take care of me." We all loved him except Mark, but I thought he was a little jealous. As for Madeline, she loved both her sons the same, but it was a long time before I realized what it meant for her to know that she was the only person in the world who felt that way.

Pyle didn't growl like an animal. He didn't sound the way a dog or a bear might, but the way a person might if people went around growling at each other. It wasn't always a mean growl, although often it was. His mean growls told you he didn't like you and you had better leave him alone. Once in a while his growling didn't seem intended to communicate anything but seemed to escape involuntarily, filled with inchoate sexuality. Still other times he growled amused growls, or impatient ones, or hungry ones. Madeline told me that he talked to her sometimes, but never when strangers were around. I'd heard him say yes and no, but not much else above a mumble. Whenever I visited The Bead Shop and customers were browsing, he growled if someone came too close to him or if he spotted someone trying to shoplift.

Jewel kept asking me whether I could get the story on Madeline in before the end of the term, but each week I'd tell her I didn't have anything yet.

"Just interview her," said Jewel. "Are you having problems?"

"No, but this is a big story," I said. "It's really big." In fact, I hadn't started writing yet. Even on hot Saturdays, I spent several hours at The Bead Shop, though Mark and everyone I knew was at the beach. Once, Mark came by looking for me and I was sitting on the floor searching through old cookie tins for coral to make a necklace with. "It's a big story," I told Mark. "I have to understand beads to do the story right."

I loved beads. I wondered what it would be like to open a place someday called "Francie's Beadorama" or "Francesca's Bead City," located in the garment district like many of the other bead or bead-and-trim shops. I knew that if I ever opened a shop it would be a plant shop, but still the bead business was something to think about. I was very egotistical so it was important to have my name on the storefront. I could open this shop far in the future, further in the future than I could imagine clearly. It was good to have lots of possibilities in mind, so you could pick and choose later.

Another reason I stopped by the shop so frequently was that Madeline was old, and I thought if she kept talking and talking, I could understand—What happens to you in life? I thought since she was old she inherently understood this and would tell me, if indirectly, simply by talking. She'd had Matt, who was thirty-six, when she was forty-six, so she was eighty-two, born in 1970. Pyle was born two years after Matt. Women routinely had babies into their fifties.

The Bead Shop was one of those places, like Mark's apartment or like that boathouse in Chicago, where I felt comfortable and serene. I fit in.

As time passed I saw I might never write this story, but I still hung around at the shop. One Saturday afternoon Mark came by and said we were going to the beach. Outside, he said, "You're getting weird."

"I like beads."

"I feel like I'm saving you from a bead cult."

Mark still hadn't gotten his car fixed, but now he'd removed the back window. That wasn't entirely voluntary. While it had been parked one day, someone had broken the glass further. So he'd had to finish the job.

As we stopped at a light I heard the couple on our right arguing. "You're crazy if you think I'm jealous," said the man. The woman said accusingly, "Then why did my psychic say you were jealous?" In front of us, a car's bumper sticker read "Honk if you're poor. Oink if you're rich." I leaned over and honked Mark's horn, and the man in front honked back. I'd seen that bumper sticker before but had never honked. I'd felt too shy. But now I felt strangely gratified. Often when I'd made deliveries in richtown, the secretaries I'd handed the deliveries to were rude or condescending to me. It wasn't anything particular they said, it was their attitude, the way they had me sit and wait and then served people who'd come after me. So I had some resentment.

The first glimpse of the ocean always surprised me, the way, when you're lying sleeplessly in bed, the first moment you realize it's getting light always surprises you. There were certain big things—love, mountains, war, the ocean—that seemed to change the value of things. When I saw the ocean, I forgot most everything else except the water.

Later, while I was lying on a state beach, there was something almost womblike the way heat touched me inside and out, and there was something dreamlike about the way people were lit as I squinted at them. The huge brown rocks in the water were incredibly lifelike—the kids sitting on them looked like elephant riders. I closed my eyes and lay on my back.

"That's him," said Mark urgently, poking me.

I looked up and saw James Goodman, the administrator Bernard was stalking. He was walking out of the water with a young man. There was an aura of contentedness about him, but it was a vulnerable contentedness, as if he knew how easily these things were lost. But he couldn't have known he was hunted, or that we were watching him.

"He's so skinny," I said. Without his street clothes, he was all angular ribs and bony thighs.

Mark lay back and frowned, and then his face went blank.

"Don't you think it's a conflict of interest if that guy with him is a student?" I said. "Don't you think if he's a student it's right to report him? Maybe it's in exchange for advantages."

Mark looked worried, almost pained. I think he didn't believe anything was inherently good or bad, but he believed you should live your life as if you did believe that. Or maybe what he thought was that each world did have a moral order, but there were a lot of different worlds. Sometimes I think the difference between Mark and me was that there was a region of shadows existing between different people's moral orders, and he understood that region better than I did. I never thought of Mark as good or bad, just as the way he was, and I loved the way he was.

That spring, he was making a living by selling office furniture and cabinets. One of the last big American financial companies that still had a branch in Los Angeles had gone under, and they were selling all their furniture cheap. Mark bought a bunch of two-drawer filing cabinets, hydraulic chairs, and mahogany desks, and sold everything for a profit. Now he wouldn't have to work for a few months if he didn't want to. I admired how he was always finding ways to make money, how he wasn't like everyone else. He was always alert for a new opening, and if there was an opening he filled it. As I lay on the beach, I thought about how this was one of the two best springs of my life—the other was the spring my cousins Steven and Nadine had stayed with my family in Chicago.

I was pleased to be working for a sleazebag lawyer, to be

hanging around The Bead Shop, and to be in love with Mark.
And yet in many ways—as with the months with Steven, when
my parents were just getting sick—this spring was one of the
worst of my life. I tried to keep the part of my heart where Rohn
had once resided empty, but sometimes it filled with sadness
instead.

But, still, I loved the spring. I think the first moment I knew
Mark and I were in love was two months earlier while we were
walking through a relatively new part of downtown one evening.
It was so amazing to see Mark looking at me in that love way,
to know that I owned that, there in the shadow of those great
silver buildings underneath the falling sun. I wanted to throw
what I owned up in the air, catch it, hold it, kiss it, protect it,
risk it, and kiss it again. Once, Jewel had told me that the
reason she stayed with Teddy was because she thought there
was a mansion inside his head, and when she thought she might
lose him she wanted to rip his face open and get at the mansion
inside. Another time, Teddy had told me that what he loved
about Jewel was the way it was a challenge to control her, but
it wasn't impossible. I did not want to control Mark because I
felt the more I controlled the less I would understand. I didn't
understand him at all. I think that was because I developed
prejudices about a person as quickly as I developed insights.
So sometimes I didn't seem to be getting anywhere. No doubt
that was true of everyone—people's perceptions were based on
prejudices as much as insights. But I wished it did not have to
be that way.

When I looked at Mark—those sharp cheekbones, the strong
torso, the graceful hands—I never felt I wanted to get inside
his brain. Touching was the thing. I just felt I wanted to touch
him all the time.

After the beach, we went to my place, sitting on the roof to
eat. There was a view of all sides of Los Angeles. There were

many musicians living in my building. Groups of three or four in a single small apartment. Sometimes, if they were women, an incredibly beautiful man would live with them, and if they were men, an incredibly beautiful woman would. All the musicians seemed interchangeable somehow, not just the way they dressed but their expressions and their clothes and probably even their dreams. It seemed weird to think that someday some of them might be famous. Or, maybe, none of them would. Probably none of them would.

I liked seeing the city from the roof. On the larger streets you could see buses with tinted green windows glowing, people staring through that green glow no matter what the hour. On the smaller streets, sometimes old couples wearing sweaters walked in the mild air. Once, I saw an old couple kissing by a towering plastic palm, and the sight made me happy until I had the thought that both of them were probably carrying guns of some sort for protection on their walk.

The air always smelled like honeysuckle and star jasmine, like eucalyptus and gasoline. I'd missed that smell when I was in the hospital, after the car had hit me. During the afternoon, when the pollution seemed to be peaking and the air was hazy and hot, I hated the smell of Los Angeles. But, still, it was better than the sanitized odors of the hospital. But the hospital was one of those things I couldn't think about often, because if I did I might get in the habit of thinking about it all the time. My mother always told me that someday I might regret the things I'd never done or the feelings I'd never known, but she doubted I would ever regret the things I'd never thought about. I knew she didn't believe that entirely, but I also knew that nothing would come of thinking about the hospital.

I never got tired of the view from the roof, of all that darkness and light out there.

The day we went to the state beach, Mark took a bath before

bed. I fell asleep and when I happened to wake up a couple of hours later he still hadn't come to bed. I went in the bathroom and found him breathing heavily in the tub, a beer cannister floating over his stomach, his knees bent in a coffin of water. I got scared and shook him hard. "What is it?" He looked surprised.

"I don't know, the way you looked . . ."

"How?"

"Dead."

"That's a pleasant thought." I dried him off with the towel and fixed my braid, messy from sleep, in the bathroom mirror. I always braided my hair at night because Mark wanted to see my face better as we had sex. I liked that he asked me to braid my hair, because I felt the same way he did. I wanted to see, taste, smell, feel, and hear every little thing. I loved the way his neck tasted salty on hot days, I loved the double-triangle our legs made when he entered me from behind, and I loved the way he smelled between his legs. Sometimes later, lying in bed next to him, I would feel incredibly satisfied thinking how I was there, in bed with a man the way I'd pictured it someday when I was a child. I was twelve the first time I ever longed to grow up specifically so I could have sex. That was during my other best spring ever.

In Chicago we'd lived in a red-brick apartment that I later found out had a reputation for housing a lot of drunks. There were several single mothers with young kids, and these women's boyfriends came by a lot. The other kids always seemed dirty, but later when I saw pictures of Steven and me I saw that we were dirty as well. I liked that, how we all had the freedom to be dirty when we didn't have school or company, or even if we did. I used to sit on the tan back porch. Nearly all the back porches in Chicago were then painted tan; today, I'd heard, they were all sorts of bright colors. In the evenings, I could smell beer from everybody's back porches. Sometimes our next-door neighbor's boyfriend got drunk after he and his girlfriend had quarreled, and he would come pounding on her door and screaming, "Diana-a-a-a! Diana-a-a-a!" no matter what time it was. "I love yoo-o-o-o, Diana!"

During happier times, I always sat on the back porch while they were kissing on their side of the porch. Sometimes I went through catalogues with Steven—every summer, I got to order three new dresses for school, and that year, with Steven there, I was helping him pick out his new clothes, too—even though, as it turned out, he would be gone by the time the clothes came. After he went to bed, I stayed outside pretending to read as moths flew back and forth in my light. I hated moths but tolerated them for the privilege of hearing Diana's boyfriend murmur things to her like, "You have the most fabulous tits," and "Bite me, darling, bite me."

Two stories down lived a boy I loved, Jack Martini, who used to pitch coins against the stairs with his friends. He was in eighth grade, and I used to kiss my arm and give it hickies and pretend he'd given them to me. I had hickies all over. I needed to wear long sleeves and pants so my mother wouldn't see them. I was very limber and had hickies in places you wouldn't believe. In my imagination, Jack gave me all of them. Once, one of the boys from across the courtyard came to my door and knocked and then ran away when I answered, and after that I imagined him giving me hickies, too.

Steven was seven, Nadine seventeen. She used to go to Morse Beach almost every night during the spring to meet her boyfriend, Geoffrey. Nadine, Steven, and I each had a corner of the dining room for our desks, but Nadine placed a screen around hers so no one could see in. She used booby traps—pen caps and paper clips and slips of paper placed just so—to make sure that if anyone touched anything on her desk, she would know.

I didn't know what to make of Nadine. Sometimes she was sweetly shy, other times abusive and selfish. I admired her enormously. Her boyfriend was three years older, and they belonged to the militant Youth Corps. She hardly ever talked to me or Steven, but the night Senator Schumaker of Oregon was shot, we sat up late on the couch in Nadine's room in front and all cried together. Her room was very small, with concrete floors and walls, but there were windows on three sides. It was warm, and we opened all the windows. The red brick of the apartment across the way looked black in the night. I cried because Roy Schumaker was really cute and nice and I loved him, and Steven cried because he was scared. Nadine cried because she loved him and she was scared, both.

The next day after school Steven and I walked home together. A lot had happened. On a street near home, there had been three fires—one in a grocery, another in a laundry, and the third in a pawn shop. Two of the fires were still smoldering, wisps of smoke blowing upward. The pawn shop had already cooled off. I'd gone into the shop once in a while. The owner, a huge, bellicose man named Davis, was standing outside. Davis wasn't his first name, or his last name. It was just his name.

"What happened?" I said.

"There was a fire," he said. He wasn't trying to be smart. He seemed so tired that that was all he could say.

"I guess somebody did this because of Schumaker," said someone in the crowd.

"Schumaker," Davis boomed. I liked it when he talked loudly, because I knew it was just for show. "What happened to him is the symptom, not the cause."

The person nodded in agreement. (Later, when I told Nadine what Davis said, she said it wasn't true, that some people weren't just symptoms, they caused things, and that's what made them special.)

It was ninety-five out that day; ash stuck to Davis's sweaty face. There was a crowd at each fire, workers from nearby stores and kids out from school. Mostly people were at the other, still-smoldering fires. All of a sudden Davis started yelling as loudly as he could: "Take anything you want! Free the people! Take anything you want!" He reached his arms heavenward, so I thought he was talking to God. He looked at the kids milling about. He was talking to us! And then there were kids every-where, all of us yelling and running toward his store. We made such a commotion that the ash soared around us and colored the sunbeams gray. Parts of the floor were wet from the firemen's hoses. None of us could stop coughing for a moment, but we all held our ground. To keep the ash settled, we moved slowly, and this caused a silence and solemnity to accompany our search. I picked out a damp magazine for my father, a canvas bag, a barette, and a guitar with no strings. Steven chose seven pipes.

My parents were still at work when we arrived home. Nadine, who'd been at her desk-fort, peeked out and was aghast when she saw us. I looked in a mirror and saw my face striped with ash and sweat. Steven's hands, clothes, and face were black. Nadine made us take a bath and I cleaned our clothes in the sink—the water swirled black. Steven and I had our beds in the living room, opposite each other. That night after he got in bed, he offered me one of his pipes. I said he should keep them, and he closed his eyes, then opened them and studied his pipes critically, then got up and arranged them perfectly in a row on the end table before he went to sleep for good.

My parents went out that night to a friend's, and Geoffrey came over and stayed very late. I woke up to hear Nadine and him having sex in her room. They were making the most amazing grunts and breathing sounds. At times I couldn't distinguish who was making which sound. I rolled up my sleeve and gave myself a hickey. Afterward, their soft voices sounded like no voices I'd ever heard, like angels' voices. When I woke up they were gone.

Over the next few weeks, sometimes Nadine was happy and would even let Steven and me into her desk-fort, but other times she would cry in bed at night. That was usually after she and Geoffrey had fought, and she hadn't seen him in several days. I never said anything when I heard her in her room crying, but finally one night I got up and knocked on her door.

"Nadine?"

"What."

"Why are you crying?"

"Shut up."

Then I was mad. "You too."

As usual, when I woke up she was gone.

When the Independent Party convention came at the end of August, there were bus, taxi, and subway strikes in Chicago. Nadine went to Grant Park, where the demonstrations were, every night. Though the convention was miles away, my mother and my friends' mothers made us all come in for good every afternoon. By the third day of the convention, the city had imposed a nighttime curfew for grownups as well as minors. I looked down the street from our fourth floor apartment one evening. It was still light out, but the street was empty of cars and people. The orange sun reflected off the buildings down the street, making the façades look like dull brass. Televisions flickered in the windows of the apartments across the way. We watched the convention coverage on our own TV. A newscaster in a suit asked a man with long hair, "What exactly does your hairstyle represent?" and the man swung to punch at him but missed.

I couldn't sleep later on. I kept thinking of how intense and hopeful Nadine's face was every night before she went out.

She came home very late, with Geoffrey. They went into her room, which because of the windows was the worst room in the house during winter but the best during spring and summer.

"Are we going or not?" Geoffrey said.

"Whatever. Are you sure they're home?"

"Look, I told you they were home. The question is, do you want to go?"

"You're always bossing me around."

"I'm not bossing you," he said patiently. "I'm asking if you want to go out. I'm asking, all right. I'm asking."

I don't really know what was going on those days. Maybe they were falling out of love but didn't want to. Maybe they were falling more in love and couldn't handle it. He walked through the living room and into the kitchen to make a phone call. When I heard his voice I got up to talk to Nadine.

"Are you okay?" I said.

"What are you doing up?" She paused. "Are *you* okay?"

I tried to think, Was I okay? "Actually, I'm going bald. Yesterday I counted. There were thirty-nine hairs in the drain after my shower, and there are hairs all over the house. I *might* need a doctor." I added that last dramatically.

"Maybe you're molting," she said dryly. Her black hair shone even in the dark. Though the shadows hid her face, I could tell she was crying and trying to hide it. We studied the empty street together.

"In a few months, no one will even remember all this," she said. She said that in the future, because of things that had happened that year, the world would be changed from then on. She said it would be as if light suddenly started to reflect at a slightly different angle off of surfaces, everywhere all at once. "Everything would look different, shadows and so on, but no one would notice."

"Nadine." Geoffrey was beside us.

"Uh-huh." Her voice was suddenly hopeful.

"I'm gonna get going," he said. I was standing between them, and they talked over my head.

"Geoff, I'm sorry."

"Yeah, I know," he said. "But, you know, it's getting late."

Nadine put her arm around me and squeezed tight. "We don't care. Francie and I were having a very nice chat, and you can do whatever you want."

Geoffrey's footsteps sounded louder when he left than they had when he'd entered the room a minute earlier, and then the door slammed.

Nadine put on the jacket that had been tied around her waist.

"Are you going to follow him?" I said.

"I'm going for a walk."

"Can I come? Please please please. Mom and Dad are asleep."

She thought a brief moment before her face took on a why-not inspiration. "Get a jacket."

I put on tennis shoes and a jacket, and we walked to Morse Beach. It wasn't close, but it was a lovely evening for walking. I recognized a few of Nadine's friends at the beach, but most of the people were strangers. The beach was quite cool. At times I felt overwhelmed by the wind and by smells from all over, and other times when the wind stopped, I could smell only the small world around me. The waves pushed up against a line of dead alewives on the sand.

A man walked up. "Nice outfit," he said to me. "Very comfortable looking." My pajamas were pink and baggy. He picked up a lock of my hair and sniffed at it. I didn't move, and he leaned over and I felt his teeth on my neck. I thought I felt his teeth all the way down to my toes.

Nadine socked him so hard he reeled backward and almost tripped. "She's eleven years old."

One of Nadine's friends had brought food—tamales, reconstituted milk, and sodas. I felt ravenous and ate four tamales, then stuck out my stomach and inflated it like a balloon. Everyone laughed. One of the guys tweaked my nose and I fell in love with him. He showed me a chokehold the police used, and after he'd trapped me on the sand, Nadine leaned down and said, "If it was for real, you'd poke him in the eye, sweetie."

They went to wade in the water and left me alone. I dropped a tamale into a milk carton and poured sand and soda in and mashed it all together with a stick. I shook the carton until when I reopened it, it was too disgusting inside for me to want to play with anymore. A cool wind blew at my face. There was a feeling in the air of something ending. Maybe it was a season ending, or maybe it was a period of history ending. Whatever, I felt a thin layer of melancholy, of fatigue and disappointment, spread over the grass and sand and water. Yet I felt happy, too, to be out there in the wind in the middle of the night. I sat for a long time waiting for Nadine. Finally she came and sat by me, seeming tense and excited, the way she might if she'd just had a long long cry. There were groups of people all around us, and several couples lay in the grass or sand. Nadine caught sight of one of the couples and her face fell. Her whole body seemed to deflate somewhat. That was the first time I ever saw the face of someone whose heart was breaking.

"Forget him," I said. "His breath stinks."

She was crying, and she grabbed my arm and pulled me around so hard that I was facing the water. Her fingers seemed to be digging past my muscles and into my bones. "Look at this." She gestured with her arm. Her arm was shaking, as if it, too, were crying. "Look at the water. And look at this." She whacked an empty milk carton and it went flying. She pushed my face down so that my nose touched the sand. "Look at the sand." My eyes felt crossed. "Don't forget anything that happened this year, or any year ever. But especially this year. Remember every sad and happy thing," she said, "because it's who you are."

Heat

Because he'd been sick for a couple of weeks, Matt didn't attend his rally and no one had talked to him lately. About a hundred students marched around for a while, down to the local police station and back. Across the street about fifty people marched to protest against expanding a commercial zone at the expense of housing. They threw smoke bombs on the freeway, bringing traffic to a halt, and then they scattered. At first we were busier watching them than running our own protest. The heat was enervating, very dry so you felt parched and crispy rather than sweaty. Once, I saw Mark staring dazedly at an upside-down sign someone was dragging. "What are you looking at so intently?" I said.

"I was just thinking."

"About what?" I looked at the sign. There was a picture of Matt wearing his hair loose, curly wisps falling around his neck.

"That guy's not right. There's something wrong."

"Why do you say that?"

"I think the only reason people care about him is they're not sure whether he *did* kill someone. That's what makes him interesting."

"It's the heat. It's making you think nutty."

Mark squinted up at the sun. There was a major smog alert that day, and the sky was dirty blue with faded violet clouds. "Yeah," he said dreamily. "Sure, the heat."

After the rally I went to see Madeline, who'd invited me over for supper. She lived in an old stucco tract house on the edge of Dogtown northeast of downtown Los Angeles. You could see the downtown skyline through a huge building that was being built, with just the metal structure completed. It was like looking at the city through a cage.

Outside Madeline's yard were faded cannas and parched banana plants. Inside, half the living room floor was covered with newspapers in piles several feet high. Pyle sat watching TV, mostly a baseball game. But he changed channels frequently, sometimes back and forth repeatedly between a couple of stations.

"Come into the kitchen," said Madeline. "I'm almost done cooking. Do you like cornbread?"

"I love it. It smells great."

An oscillating fan blew on us. It was one of those fans that changed direction and power in accordance with the temperature it sensed. But it seemed to be broken, and the air by the oven was still and warm. The temperature was supposed to break a record the next day, reaching 119°. The previous record, set in

1997 and matched the previous year, was 115°. Today was 110°.

"How did the rally go?"

"Very well, I guess. But I was so hot that it was hard to jump around and get excited. We marched down to the police station and back and had a rally in the quad."

"I wish I could have been there, but I just finished selling my shop today."

"Congratulations."

She opened the oven and took out the cornbread.

"Is Matt eating with us? Is he here? I heard he's been sick."

"He's better. He's going back to his place today. He's been staying here."

Pyle came into the kitchen to join us. She smiled at me. "I don't even have to call him. He hears the oven opening and closing." Pyle sat down and started eating, ignoring us. Madeline closed her eyes. She looked very sucked out from the heat, and I felt alarmed. It seemed that one moment she'd been fine, the next sick. Then I realized her eyes were closed because she was praying. Her lips moved and her eyeballs rolled. I closed my eyes and said—and meant—"Thank you."

"Dig in," she said.

Pyle used his tongue as much as his teeth as he ate. I loved to watch certain people eat. I found it moving, I didn't know why. And he was one of those people. Once, I reached over to get the salt, near his plate. He growled a small, tight growl and put up his hand, as if to protect his plate from intrusion.

"He loves to eat," Madeline said. "Sports, eating, and bright things like certain beads. Those are his three loves." She pushed the cornbread closer to him.

"He can follow sports?"

"He understands them perfectly well," she said, annoyed.

The cornbread was heavy and hard, but I liked heavy food. We were not gourmets in my family. Pyle reached out and took the rest of the cornbread—five pieces—and put it on his plate. Matt had just walked into the room. "Put that back," he said. He turned to me and shyly said, "Sorry."

"That's okay, I have plenty." We both looked at my plate, which was empty, and then we both blushed.

Matt started rearranging the fan and opening and closing the various windows and curtains. He opened one a half an inch, another two inches, and closed one an inch and a half. "Air currents," he muttered. He seemed distracted by the concepts he was putting to work, but I got the feeling that at the same time he was observing me.

"I was at your rally today. It was pretty low-key without you."

"It was hot, and he hasn't been well," Madeline put in.

"I don't really like being the center of attention," said Matt. He shook his curly hair distractedly with his hands, then turned to his mother. "I'm going to get going."

"Okay, hon, I'll talk to you later."

He politely said good-bye to me, and in a few minutes a car started and drove off. I had the feeling he'd been waiting around to hear how the rally went but that he didn't want me to know it.

Madeline went to bed after supper, so I cleaned up the kitchen. Pyle seemed to have accepted my presence the way he might have accepted a new plant or a pet fish in the house. While he returned to his game on television, I emptied the ice trays and put the ice in bowls in the freezer, then I filled the trays with water. I don't know why I didn't leave. I felt as if I were preparing for a siege, a siege of what I didn't know—heat or sickness or both. Though there was no reason to stay, I made myself at home. For a while Pyle and I watched television. Every time I moved, he growled slightly without looking my way. Finally he fell asleep, snore-growling. I checked in a back hallway and could hear Madeline snoring from her room. At the other end of the bedroom hall, I pushed at a door and turned on the lights. Sports memorabilia covered the walls. There were posters of home-run hitters with bats resting on their shoulders and of quarterbacks kneeling with footballs. There were pennants, and blankets with baseball caps all over them. Sports, bright things, and food. A bowl of bright brass beads sat atop a sort of shrine to quarterback Gordie Gordon.

I don't know what I was looking for or why I felt it was my business to look at all. I'd just thought tonight would be my last opportunity to open this door. I closed it now.

Back in the living room again, I curled up on a chair. This place felt like the opposite of one of my safe spots, or like a false safe spot. When I was going to grade school in Chicago, during riot drills we were supposed to kneel against a wall with our coats over our heads, holding hands with our drill partners. We were supposed to keep a coat at school, no matter what the weather. I always felt my teacher was protecting me and I was safe. I felt this even though crazy Mrs. Winter who used to snap the girls' bra straps in sixth grade ("You're too young!") once told us that if we were ever outside and saw "a group of angry people approaching," we were supposed to throw ourselves under a car, and if there were no cars around, we should fling ourselves through the nearest window. I still felt safe. But safe from what? A riot that never came, and if it did come, I wouldn't have been safe from it under a car or kneeling against a wall holding hands with my best friend. So, was I feeling safe from what did exist or from what didn't? That's sort of the way I felt that night at the Burroughs' house, as if something was happening—here or in the world, I didn't know—that no one could prevent, that no one was safe from.

Pyle got up and went to bed, ignoring me. I fell asleep on the couch and woke up later to the sound of a truck whirring, moving up and down through a grocery store parking lot across the street. They must have been cleaning the lot. The truck whirred on. I fell asleep again and dreamed people in a big whirring tank were trying to kill me and my friends, and I had to kill the other people to protect us. My dreams never soothed me. They were always tests, of my courage, of my ethics. And always I failed. I had to fail, because if I killed the people trying to hurt us I'd failed by killing, and if I didn't kill them I failed by not protecting my friends, a higher cause for me.

I woke just as it was getting light. The pinkish mist that often colored the night sky in Los Angeles was just fading and leaving behind a slate-blue sky. The view, which I found strangely appealing, included the supermarket, a Chinese restaurant, and an empty coin-op laundromat that was all yellow and orange inside, with a red vending machine lit up just inside the door. The heat was surreal. I almost felt I was on another planet. Everything was peaceful. After checking on Madeline, who was still snoring, and Pyle, nestled among his bright things and sports treasures, I went outside to leave. It turned out to be no cooler outside than in. Even my car was warm inside, not cool from the night. The motor sounded loud in the quiet.

I opened all the windows. At a stop light near a park, I heard singing and saw two flashlights lying in the grass. Then, as if they'd just materialized, I saw several people sitting together. They were singing a ragged version of "Oh, Beautiful," which the Green Party used in lieu of the national anthem at conventions and official functions. Palm trees stretched high all around them. Hardly anyone voted Green, but they'd pulled a steady two percent of the voters for the last decade.

I always felt insulated in my small old car even when I had all the windows open. So I was surprised when two men approached, one on each side, and said they liked my car and would pay me seven dollars to drive them a couple of blocks up the road. I stepped on the accelerator and went through the red, just missing someone crossing my path. I didn't know why they hadn't just jumped in and taken the car. I never understood the lines people drew, why they would do one thing but not another.

The sky was getting light. As I drove through Koreatown, I saw an old woman hurrying into a van with "Korean Christian Church" printed on the side. A couple of miles north, toward Hollywood, I passed two men wrestling in front of an all-night taco stand. In Hollywood, three prostitutes walked confidently down the street. I didn't want to stop. The car didn't have air conditioning, but with the wind blowing through the windows, I knew I was cooler than I would be in my apartment. Finally, around seven, my fuel light lit up and I stopped at a coffee shop not far from school. I didn't have any gas credits left. I was going to have to take the bus for the rest of the week.

Sometimes someone from school was at the coffee shop, but it was empty now. I felt lonely. When the waitress came for my order, I talked and talked to her about any insipid thing I could think of while she tried to politely extricate herself. Someday I was going to be one of those old people who couldn't stop talking to you in line at the Fedcal supermarket.

I had to be at work for the lawyer this morning at nine, so around eight I started getting up. His office was only half an hour away by car, but longer by bus. I saw Joe walking toward the coffee shop. I waited for him. He came in and collapsed at my booth.

"Hi," I said.

"Hi." His face was waxy with perspiration and oil. He rubbed his fingers lightly over the bumps on his forehead. I noticed a hickey on his neck. I hadn't had a hickey since the last time I gave myself one. I smiled and raised my eyebrows at his neck. "Oh, that," he said. He turned to look out the window, wiping at his neck as if trying to wipe his hickey off. He didn't turn away from the window, even when the waitress came for his order. I asked for iced coffee for him. He was staring at the sky. It was only slightly windy, but a white grocery bag was floating high above the ground, the black and red writing on it rippling slowly. My hand lay in the window, and every time I rested it too long, my bracelets started to heat up. Joe didn't speak. It was eerily quiet, the way it always seemed to be during extremes in weather. Once, in Chicago, it was twenty below zero, and the city turned into an empty world of hard things—ice and concrete and brick—and no sounds at all.

The waitress set his coffee down. "Here's a drink for you," I said.

He turned absently to his coffee and glugged the whole thing down at once, some of it dripping on his chin. He wiped his chin, also absently, and shook the ice in the cup a couple of times.

"I have to be getting going in a second," I said. "I have work today."

He said, "I went out with Patricia the other day."

"The girl from the sub shop?"

He nodded.

"How did it go?"

He shrugged in a who-cares way. "Ah, she's a prostitute. She got makeup all over my shirt. I hope it washes out. A *prostitute*."

"I'm sorry." The air between us suddenly filled with awkwardness. "Did you like her?" I said idiotically.

"No," he said. "I mean, no, don't be sorry." He got a surprisingly wistful look in his eyes, and then, for the first time since I'd known him, his innocent face was full of pain. "Yeah to the other question. I liked her. I really liked her a lot. I loved her. I really loved her. But I guess I won't be seeing her again unless I can come up with five hundred dollars. That was about a quarter of my savings. Maybe I'll call her every time I get two thousand saved." Two thousand was barely enough to pay one month's rent in the scummiest shoebox of an apartment. His face suddenly lit up. "She seemed to like me." He looked at me as if for affirmation.

And seeing his face alight that way, I thought that it was quite possible that she did like him, and that in any case five hundred dollars was not too much to pay for that look. "I'm sure she did," I said.

His wistfulness returned and was still there when I left him.

At work, my boss was going crazy. I swear it was the heat, changing him and his clients. He was losing all of them lately. These days every time he bagged a new client, he exclaimed, "America, I love you!" But he hardly ever bagged any anymore, and two former clients had filed malpractice suits against him. When he didn't answer us on the intercom, one of the other assistants and I walked into his office and found him sitting in his chair with his lunch all dismantled in front of him on his desk. He'd taken his sandwich apart, and arranged the bread and Meat-Ex in a four-piece square. He looked at us thoughtfully. "Why don't one of you girls take off all your clothes and feed me snacks?" he said.

"Sure," said the other woman. "And why don't you give me a big fat raise?" To me she said, "I guess it's time to find a new job."

In my head, I quit right then.

I went to my desk and took out my notes on Madeline. I realized I didn't have much information on her. I knew what kind of plants she kept in her yard, how many bedrooms her house had. But after all the time I'd spent with her, I hadn't managed to gather many facts about her and Matt and what his troubles meant to her. I hadn't obtained even one decent quote about his situation. I knew I would never get any such quotes. She'd looked awful the night before, dry and hollow. When I called her home, nobody answered. I sat there—*waiting*—and in a couple of hours Mark called and said Matt had found her dead.

"Will you come by and get me?" I asked. "I was running low on fuel and left my car somewhere."

"Where were you? I called last night."

"I stayed at Madeline's."

"All right, just let me tie some things up here. Did you want to go out to her house or something?"

"Yeah."

My boss was standing at the door with his lunchbag. Paper bags were more prestigious than cloth ones, which is what I always used. Stores made you pay for paper or plastic bags. "Would you like a snack?" my boss said.

"I'm giving notice," I said. "I'm quitting."

"When are you quitting?"

"When my boyfriend gets here."

He walked off mumbling, "Nobody wants any snacks."

When Mark arrived, we drove out to the Burroughs' place. As soon as we walked to the door, a neighbor hurried up to me. "Can I help you?" she said.

"I'm not sure. I knew the family."

"She just passed away."

"I know." The heat made it difficult for me to breathe.

"I talked to her just a couple of weeks ago, can you imagine? My son told me she didn't look well, but I thought she seemed fine. When my first husband passed away, it was the same thing, such a surprise. He'd always been in perfect health, he never complained. A very happy man, and one day he had a stroke and died. It surprised everyone. You really can't tell. If you can't tell with your own husband, who can you tell with?"

"Do you know what happened to her sons?"

She leaned forward conspiratorially. "The one came by and took the other away. What was his name? Kyle?"

"Pyle."

"They're going to put him in a home. Madeline always told me that. The sale of the house is going to pay for his keep. It was sold a long time ago, but the agreement was she could live there until she died. And then of course she sold the store."

"Of course," I said. "Do you happen to know which home?"

"This one. They sold it to two families who plan to live there together. Neither could afford a house on their own."

"I mean, which home is Pyle in?"

"The Sherwood, or Sherbourne, something like that. The Sher-something Halfway House." She became suddenly alert. "You're Maddy's friend? I always called her Maddy."

"I went to school with her son Matt."

A man came out and she turned to him. "This young lady says she went to school with Matt."

"Ohhh," he said. He, too, leaned toward me. "Then I guess you heard about his troubles."

"We didn't really like him living next to us," his wife said.

A phone started ringing and they looked at me as if annoyed I'd been holding them up. When they'd gone in, Mark and I found a pay phone and I made some calls to find Pyle's halfway house. It turned out to be called the Sureway Halfway House, in West Los Angeles. Mark's tank was halfway empty, but it was plenty to get across town.

The Sureway looked just like any large apartment complex from the outside. Inside a large lobby, some people, mostly fairly young, were watching TV. Someone in a reception area told me Pyle was in an art class now, and she pointed me in the direction. "Already in a class?" I said, but she didn't reply.

He wasn't there, though, just several people scribbling lethargically on large pieces of newsprint. The teacher smiled at me and said proudly, "Lorraine drew this in response to a friend's suicide. Lorraine, show this nice lady your picture." Lorraine glared at me and held up her picture, a bunch of green and black lines. Perhaps I was just imagining things, but I thought those lines looked extremely mean. The teacher said, "It represents Lorraine's desire to live." She told me Pyle was probably up in his room, and pointed in the direction. "The rooms are that way. I'm not sure where his is."

It didn't matter. I found him sitting in the shade on a bench in the courtyard. He looked the same as ever, golf shirt and creased slacks. I wondered who would crease his slacks now. I sat next to him and he glanced at me without recognition. He didn't growl. I missed that. Maybe somebody had already made him stop doing that.

"Hi," I said.

He looked at what he had in his lap, a collection of metal beads, very shiny, that were all strung together.

"They're pretty." He didn't acknowledge me. Someone was watching us from an upstairs window, but then I saw she wasn't watching us at all. She was just sort of watching, in general. A gardener worked in a corner, sweeping dirt, shining plastic leaves.

"Do you like those beads?" I said.

"Yes," he said, and my heart jumped as he answered me.

"You do? You like beads?"

"No. Yes."

I paused. "What's your name?"

"Yes." I wondered whether, even after years and years of knowing better, Madeline's heart had jumped every time he spoke a word or two, and then broke every time she realized he wasn't really responding to anything she'd said. I didn't know what to do. I gave him all the money in my pockets—eighteen dollars—and Mark and I left him with his bright things. It was getting dark. We sat in the car. There were three cats sitting in the middle of the road, and beyond them a traffic light that seemed to stay red forever. A man, chubby with a green shirt, was spinning slowly in a sort of dance down the street. His arms were akimbo, his hair was long and matted. He stopped to shake his hips in front of a woman with a baby in a stroller. The woman pointed a gun at him, and he twirled on. It was hard to watch crazy people sometimes, because whenever I saw them I felt what I was seeing was pain, or, really, something beyond pain. It wasn't that I thought pain had caused them to go crazy, I thought it was painful not to be able to communicate. I'd never been in that realm beyond pain. But when I felt myself near there, I cried and cried. Otherwise I tried never to cry. When I did, eventually I would wonder, Where do tears come from? Why does my body heave when I cry? I'd start to have curiosity about the process of crying, and I'd know that everything was going to be okay.

"Where did you leave your car?" said Mark.

"By that coffee shop at Vermont and Russell."

He started the engine.

It seemed to me that Madeline had done everything she could for her sons, yet how much had she really changed?

"I'll be right back," I said, and jumped out to the sidewalk.

Back in the reception room, I asked the woman working there whether Matt Burroughs had left his address.

"Who's Matt?"

"The guy who brought Pyle Burroughs in. It's his brother."

"A woman brought him in."

"Are you sure?"

"Yes, she said she was a friend."

"Did she leave a name or address?"

The receptionist shook her head no.

"Are you sure?"

For an answer her nostrils flared and she looked down at her work.

I returned to the car. There had been a couple more smoke bombs dropped on freeways that day, so we took surface streets. Mark took Wilshire, with its towering office buildings, down to Highland Avenue, then east on Beverly Boulevard. I liked the part of Beverly that curved between two halves of a golf course. Because the course had been built on a filled-in swamp, the air at night was often humid, causing frequent fogs. The heat had finally broken. The fog tonight was low and thick, almost liquid, moving lava-like over the road. When my parents had died, shortly after straightening out their affairs—and in the process, my affairs—my aunt told me that she believed certain people under certain conditions could keep themselves alive for an extra week or month or even longer, in order to finish taking care of the futures of the people they loved. "It's a type of levitation," she said. I opened the window, smelled the musty air. If I ever wrote a story on Madeline Burroughs it ought to have just one sentence: "She practiced levitation."

Insolence

"You were named Francie because your parents had a good friend who came from France, but at the end they hated her guts. My brother Bob hates his name and makes his wife call him Gus when they're in bed. I could change my name tomorrow if I wanted. Movie stars change their names all the time. But the point I'm trying to make is, who are we all trying to kid?"

I had no idea what Mark was talking about, but he was in an agitated mood, so I sat back and let him talk, the most practical thing to do when he was feeling this way. He accelerated around the curve of the on-ramp. That was one of the things he'd taught me, how you're supposed to accelerate around curves, not brake. It made the car hug the road better. Mark's face seemed suddenly helpless. "Let's see . . . What else can I give commentary on?" His eyes caught fire. "Human beings! Ants!" he cried out. And indeed, the swarm of tiny cars moving around us did seem buglike. We were driving on the Harbor Freeway, straight through the middle of downtown, skyscrapers all around us, their logos red, orange, blue, and white against a surprisingly white sky with black clouds. It was strange, to see all that color against black and white, and to see the sky so white though it was late.

Mark looked at me mock-critically. "Honey, you should always wear your hair in rollers like that. I mean it, you're a lemonade stand in the Saudi desert." He laughed then, and I couldn't help laughing too, because he spoke affectionately. That was what was different about him from every other guy I'd ever known, which actually wasn't that many guys. When you looked silly, it didn't bother him at all. He liked people when they looked silly because it made them raw and vulnerable and without protection.

"Oh, baby, baby, baby," he said. He turned on the radio but almost immediately whacked it off, probably because the person singing had been a pudgy man with an okay voice. Mark didn't believe in okay-ness, and he didn't believe in pudginess. You had to be either fat or thin. He was getting thinner lately, and he'd had his black hair chopped short so that it stuck straight up. He was agitated today because the semester was almost over and he still hadn't decided what to do this fall. His black eyes lately showed you everything or nothing that he was feeling.

"What's wrong with rollers? Since when are you a fashion consultant?"

"I'm just practicing. I'm trying to add to my collection of money-making skills."

"You're missing the turn-off," I said, and he accelerated

hard and shoved the car across two lanes to get to the Hollywood Freeway. We were coming from a sale he'd just made near his home, in the Pico-Union section. One of the recurring ways he made money was by searching the *Weekly Market*, a newspaper filled with nothing but classifieds, as soon as it came out, and then buying up bargains and reselling them for more. He bought and sold everything: musical instruments, pets, furniture, clothes. Sometimes when he sold items, he pushed the buyer hard on the price, but other times he agreed to a trade of goods or sold things for little more than he'd paid. He was generous that way to some people. Mark got his customers through referrals, and ads he tacked up here and there. Also, he sold junk to other people who sold junk for a living. At his home, the floors and tabletops were covered with whatever he hadn't sold yet. He remembered how much he'd paid for everything. He was a great businessman. We were going to make another sale—we hoped—later that night. Meanwhile, we wanted to stop at my place to eat, and then go to Jewel's for an informal staff meeting. Actually, I was just an underling and this was an editors' meeting, but they were letting me attend anyhow.

At my place I opened my mailbox and found a note from Matt.

"Look," I said. "It's from Matt."

He read over my shoulder. The letter was a copy. I bet Mark would probably find one when he got home, too. It said simply, "Thank you. You made a mistake. But thank you." We read it over a few times.

"Jesus," said Mark. "Fucked-up people will always fuck you up. Always. It's a law of nature. He's skipped bail."

"Now wait a minute. We don't know what this means."

"It means he used the paper. It means what it says, that we made a mistake. It doesn't make sense to deny that."

We walked up silently. I kept reading the note to see whether

I'd missed something, though there was nothing to it. Mark and I baked some chicken legs he'd gotten for a desk he'd sold someone. We devoured the legs, biting the ends off and sucking out the marrow. You couldn't waste anything these days. My aunt said that in her day it was still fairly common for people to throw out their apple cores rather than eat them. But we'd returned to the ways of the nineteenth century—apple cores were a treat.

We took the bus to Jewel's because we were both low on creds and had a lot of necessary driving to do that week. The others were already there, Lucas and Bernard and a couple of lower editors. Jewel had a black eye that everyone was ignoring. All of them had gotten copies of Matt's letter and were discussing it. They'd already heard about Madeline's death. "You guys are jerks," said Jewel. "I always knew it. Matt pulled one over on you."

"On you, too," said Bernard.

"I killed my parents," said Lucas. We all looked at him. "I killed my parents. Now, just because I say to you that I killed my parents doesn't mean I killed them. Do you see what I mean? We don't really know what Matt has done."

"We know what happened," said Jewel.

"I think we should give him the benefit of the doubt," I said.

"Then where is he?"

"He skipped bail, that doesn't mean he committed a crime in the first place."

"All right, forget it," said Jewel. "We made a mistake but we have a lot to talk about. We only have one more issue, so let's make it a good one."

But nobody really felt like working, so we got drunk instead. Once, I went to the bathroom and when I opened the door, Jewel was in there, blood trickling from between her legs like water from a faucet. She watched curiously, almost as if that were somebody else's vagina the blood was coming from.

"Jewel, what is it?" I said.

"Get out of here!" she shouted, getting up and slamming the door in front of me. I waited outside. I knew what it probably was. I'd read in the newspaper recently that seventy percent of women under the age of forty got cervical cancer. For some reason, more younger women than older ones got it.

When Jewel emerged, she said, "Did you ever hear of knocking?"

"Did you ever hear of locks?" I said defensively. We scowled at each other. "What's wrong? What was going on?"

"I had outpatient surgery for a cervical thing and now I have my period. So with the two, it's bloody."

"How come you didn't tell anyone about the surgery?"

"I didn't think it was anyone else's business."

"Is it okay now?"

"Yeah, it was easy. The doctor says it happens to everyone. Listen, can we forget it? I want to talk about something else."

"What?"

"About what you said before about coming to the arroyo with me. Did you mean it?"

"Of course."

"Okay, I was talking to my dad. He wanted to come but I said no. But he thinks it's a good idea to go."

Mark was calling me. "Francie, we're leaving." He walked into the hallway where I stood with Jewel.

"Already?" I said.

"What do you mean? It's eight. We've been here for two hours."

"How come you haven't talked to me in two hours?" said Jewel.

"I didn't have anything to say to you," Mark said.

"If you're talking about my face, it was an accident. We were putting up a shelf. Teddy's got all these patriotic mugs and flags and other paraphernalia that he wanted on the same shelf."

"I didn't know he was patriotic," I said.

"Oh, he's very patriotic. He has a lot of good qualities," she said excitedly.

"Maybe you should get him flag pajamas so you can feel like you're sleeping with all America," Mark said.

"I don't need this, Mark. He loves me in ways you wouldn't understand."

"Jewel, he wouldn't know love if it rose up and spit in his eye."

" 'Bye, Francie, it was nice having you over," she said, and walked away from us.

Bernard, who was drunk, was going to stay on Jewel's couch for a while. Later, he and I were going to be spying one last time on the school administrator he'd been stalking.

Mark, Lucas, and I walked out to a bus stop. There were hundreds of people across the street. Not rioters, workers. There were a number of corners in Los Angeles where people who needed laborers could go to pick them up. Every time a car drove up to one of those corners, day or night, the workers swarmed around.

"I remember doing that," said Lucas. We sat at the bus stop and watched the crowd.

"Have you gotten work that way?" I said.

"When I first dropped out of my gang."

"Did you make any money?"

"Once in a while. Not often. I was pooah. Poor is poor, but poorer than poor is *pooah*." He stared at the swarms of men, women, and children. "God, I was lonely then," he almost whispered. He straightened his tie. "We're in luck. Here comes the bus."

Mark and I went to get his car and hurry across town to make the sale he was hoping for. I went along even though I had tests coming up next week that I could have studied for. I took my classes pass/fail when I could. Once, a literature teacher told the class an anecdote about how a famous poet's wife rose from the audience at a reading her husband was giving and held up a sign saying her husband was a lecherous, fat fool. But though I recalled the anecdote, I didn't know anything about the poet or what his name was. I mean, if you gave me a really good book about murders or dinosaurs or something, I would be up all night. But it was hard to care about school reading, because once I had read the book, I did not understand why it was so important to answer the teacher's questions. Besides, I was no longer going to school from hope but from fear. I was not going because there were classes I was interested in or things that I wanted but because there were things I did not want. For instance, I did not want to work for someone like my old boss and I did not want to be him. And in lieu of any other ideas about what to do, I kept going to school.

We took the Harbor again, this time passing where they'd started building the Century Freeway somewhere around the 1980s. They'd never finished it, so there was one of those familiar concrete half-arcs reaching over the Harbor.

Mark's car was getting as agitated as he was tonight. He had two hundred thousand miles on it, and it shook and coughed. I watched another mile click by on the odometer. "I can't believe how much mileage you have on this car. How come it still runs?"

"I guess I'm just one of those people who have a special relationship with junk," he said happily.

I turned all the way around to look backward at the downtown skyline—the blue neon flame from the gas company, the rainbow lights of the Natsumi Hotel, the rows of shining ice-blue atop the Sanwa Bank building. "It looks so dreamy."

"Honey, put your seatbelt on."

"Are we getting in an accident?"

"Who knows what the future holds?"

True. I put on my seatbelt. It was true of these selling expeditions, as well. Something unexpected happened all the time. Once, I went with Mark to see a woman he'd sold clothes to on several occasions. It turned out to be someone named Gail I'd gone to grammar school with. A former redheaded beanpole with a prominent nose, she now was a blonde with a button nose and enormous breasts. Though she lived in a spartan studio with a roommate, she dressed extravagantly when we saw her, and Mark said she always dressed up. We'd been friends in Chicago when we were twelve. We had the same birthday, and our mothers got together and bought us identical "beauty kits"— zippered pouches with lip gloss, alcohol-based cleansing lotion, and gel blush. My cousin Steven poured my cleansing lotion into a bowl and set it on fire, and it burned like one of those desserts in restaurants.

The next year, when the girls at school started developing breasts, we all used to pull on our nipples when we could because the most popular girl in class—a surprising-looking Irish-Mexican girl with dark skin and red hair—had told everyone this would make them stick out more. Having nipples that stuck out was highly desirable because then boys could see them through your blouse, and also boys would have something to get hold of someday. The whole afternoon and morning before my first date ever, I pulled my nipples so vigorously that all during my date I needed to walk bent over slightly so that my breasts wouldn't rub against any material. If the boy actually had touched me I probably would have howled and slapped him.

Gail and I talked about these things and kept laughing, but then she pushed at her breasts and said brightly, "I've had these done four times so far." She looked down at them proudly and I wished we could all start over again. I mean, her breasts looked fine and everything, but they'd probably looked fine before too.

Now we drove down Central. Sprouting from the dark sidewalks, small groups of people stood laughing and talking. On a side street, a girl and a boy were kissing passionately in the middle of the road. They were skinny and small, probably not more than ten or eleven, and seeing them made me feel aged and full of wisdom. On Central, there were three boarded-up shops in a row, then a church in what looked like a former shop. The church was a small, plain, tan building with only one small window in front. The only identification was a hand-lettered sign with the name of the church on it. A man was standing outside peering into the window. Further on, a giant man filled the doorway of an all-night gas station shop, seemingly unable to decide where he might go next.

Those were the only people I saw. On another side street, the house we finally stopped at was incongruously lovely with a cloud of extremely well-made fake deciduous trees out front, and storybook red eaves. And bars on the windows, as there were on the glass windows of probably every house in the country, and certainly in the county. Plastic wasn't yet a viable alternative for most people, because it scratched too easily and needed to be replaced too often to be economical. Besides, it wasn't as beautiful as glass.

A man opened the door and nodded to Mark, barely glancing at me. A lot of people Mark dealt with were like that. Some of them spoke politely to me only if they thought I could influence Mark about the price of an item. This man, named Jason, handed Mark a beer and said, "Does she want one, too?"

"No, thank you," I said.

He kept looking at Mark. "My wife drinks a lot of beer and now she's fat," he said with disgust.

"Yeah." Mark was opening guitar cases. The front room was full of stuff, just like Mark's place was lately. A cat leaped on top of a beautiful drop-leaf table, and Jason picked it gently off, talking baby talk. I heard a woman crying in a back room, moaning in a soft, animal way between sobs.

"Francie," said Mark.

"Oh, sorry." I handed him the guitar I'd carried in.

Jason took one of the guitars and plugged it into an amplifier and played a minute. He shook his head with satisfaction. "This is a tasteful guitar. That's important. I believe at some point evil and bad taste become the same thing."

"That's my motto," said Mark cheerfully.

Jason played for about ten minutes, at first in a show-offy way, but after a while I knew that, to him, we weren't even there anymore. The cat was eating from a paper plate on the floor and I noticed there was a small plate of cat food in every corner of the room.

Jason shook his head again. "I feel sexy when I play sometimes." He played a few notes lovingly. I could hear the happy click in Mark's brain he got whenever he knew he'd made a sale. Jason seemed to sense the click and decided to try to keep the price down. "It's a nice guitar but it has some things wrong with it. For instance, it has a slight buzz sometimes."

Mark kicked me lightly. "I didn't hear a buzz," I said.

Jason gestured eagerly around the room. "Anything you interested in? Hey! I've got some kittens." Before we could answer, he'd rushed out of the room. In the back of the house he asked someone, presumably the woman who'd been crying, where the kittens were, and she replied, "It's indifferent to me." Jason returned with a box of five kittens. He set down the box and picked up two kittens in each of his hands. He held them out, two under my nose and two under Mark's. "Buy one," he pleaded.

Mark seemed to be deciding something. He turned to me wearily. "All right, is there anything around here you want?"

I looked around the living room. "I don't know. I guess that green lamp is okay."

"Sold!" cried out Jason. Mark sold him a guitar for what he'd hoped to sell it for, minus the price of the lamp. When we left, the crying had resumed, and Jason, surrounded by kittens, was standing looking lost in the middle of his living room.

Mark dropped me off at the apartment where we'd once spied on James Goodman. Bernard should have been there by now if he'd ever made it out of Jewel's.

I found him where Mark and I had waited last time. He'd told me he called Goodman a few days earlier, saying he knew what was going on. There was a possibility, he'd said, that Goodman was stealing money from the school. That excited us, the thought that we might catch someone here who was also stealing money. I felt like a lioness stalking prey.

Bernard was one of those people who couldn't help talking loudly. You could tell him to speak more softly, and he would, but then as he kept talking, his voice would get louder and louder until it returned to its original volume. I lay sleepily and contentedly in the grass, listening to his loud voice talk about what a great story this was going to be. Bernard's head jerked, and he stood up excitedly. I jumped up. Bernard stepped forward and held out his hand, saying simply, "I'm Bernard Thomas, editor of the *Campus News*."

Goodman had started at the sight of us. At the hello, he'd begun to smile, but at "editor of the *Campus News*," a new expression swallowed his face. I have a feeling my expression changed, too, after I saw his change. He just looked so caught, but also as if he'd been waiting to be caught. He broke into a run, hesitated, and ran after all. We rushed after him as far as the street, Bernard snapping pictures clumsily as we ran, but we stopped at the street when it was clear he'd outdistanced us. He started loping now, not really running hard. I thought later that he kept running not because he thought we might be chasing him, but because he wanted to feel free for a bit, to feel elevated and happy. I wanted to yell "Run!" at him, the way my mother had once yelled at me after I'd stolen that girl's purse at a carnival. Now I felt confused. The whole confrontation had been absurd rather than dramatic.

Two days later, on the Friday the final issue of the semester came out, there was no story about Goodman in the paper. Bernard told me that Goodman was dead. Apparently, he'd shot himself in his study the night we saw him. His wife had found him with a note that said, "I can't." Bernard had had a brief, curt conversation with her.

Bernard made me promise not to tell anyone we'd seen him a couple of nights earlier. "It'll only hurt his wife," he said, though we both knew we didn't want to tell anyone because his death would seem like our fault. Of course, I'd already told Mark, but I agreed not to tell anyone else. I knew I was failing myself somehow by agreeing. I had a weird feeling, a feeling like cold air seeping into a warm room. I felt that no matter what happened in the future, no matter what lives I saved or what beautiful children I raised, no matter how hard I worked and what I achieved, no matter what, a part of me would always be right here in this moment. Bernard walked away, leaving me standing in the middle of the city room. I followed him into his cubicle.

"I feel like it's wrong not to tell anyone," I said.

He chewed on that for a moment. "You can't bring back the dead."

"You can do anything you want." My voice rose shrilly.

"Come back to me in twenty years and tell me that." His eyes were bloodshot, as if he hadn't slept all night, or maybe, I realized, as if he'd been crying.

I went into a stall in the bathroom to sit and think. All bathrooms built or updated in the last twenty-five years or so had doors that stretched from the floor to about seven feet high. The stalls were a good place to think. I wondered how many times Bernard had been struck with the same cold-air feeling I'd had, and how many times in the future it would strike me again. I thought of something I'd heard a policeman say once. There'd been a shooting on the street, and a crowd of people had gathered, as well as some TV reporters. I saw one officer raise his eyebrows to another and point at something, I wasn't sure what. The other officer said, "Don't worry. If it doesn't show on TV, it doesn't count." In this way, something that really existed also *didn't* exist.

I took out my parent-rocks and the twig from the plant Rohn and Annie had given me. I felt strangely free in that little stall, whereas if I went out I thought I'd feel trapped. I put away the twig and set my parents on a metal shelf and asked them in my head what was new. They smiled and said I couldn't imagine. I don't know how long I sat in there. At some point Jewel called for me. "Francie? Mark is looking for you."

"Okay, I'll be right there." She'd known right where to come. All of us came in here to pout sometimes.

Mark and I went to eat dinner together and literally didn't speak except for when he first asked me whether I wanted to go get some food and I said sure. He somehow already knew about Goodman's death, and he was madder at me than I'd ever seen him, though I wasn't quite sure why, since he'd known beforehand that Bernard and I were going to be stalking the administrator. He hadn't seemed mad then. I think he was so mad he felt he had to be with me, because otherwise he would hate me if we were apart, and he didn't want to hate me.

Later we drove to his place. His neighborhood was a high-density area, and often on Friday and Saturday nights the streets were so crowded with people just wanting to get out of the house that his road was impossible to negotiate in a car. We drove partly into the street, then had to back up. As we were backing up, I saw a man on the third floor of Mark's building blowing his nose onto the street, without a tissue.

Mark stopped the car and stuck his head out the window and called out, "You're a pig! You're a pig!" Then he continued backing up. I felt stung because I knew I was the one he was mad at, not the man blowing his nose.

I liked Mark's small apartment because, unlike my place or any apartment my family had ever lived in when I lived at home, it had a thermostat to control the heat. I was always adjusting and readjusting the thermostat. I felt powerful to be able to do that. While I was calibrating, Mark sat at his desk pretending to be reading.

A police helicopter started hovering so low our windows rattled. I looked out, saw the helicopter circling, the searchlight hitting me and throwing all sorts of shadows and lights into the apartment. I remember thinking for a second, without surprise, that they must have been searching for me in connection with Goodman's death. The helicopter kept circling, now shining light on the street below. The street, so full of people only minutes earlier, was eerily empty. I opened the window, leaned out. There were only two girls, insolently sitting on a squad car while police searched down the street, shining flashlights under cars. I could feel an exhilaration in the girls' insolence. The air was cool. I leaned out as far as I could, then turned inside just as Mark was looking quickly back to his reading.

Finally the helicopter lifted, and the officers in the street left. In a while there were signs of life, a few kids wandering out again. Mark was at his desk writing. It was getting late.

"What are you doing?" I said.

"Writing letters to protest some things."

"Like what?"

"Like all that helicopter noise out there, for one thing. I'm going to write everybody who makes me mad."

"You'll get arrested."

"Good."

"Plus, if you really did write everyone who made you mad, you'd run out of paper."

"Then I'll run out of paper. Go to bed, okay?"

I felt stung again, but also mad at him. I got in bed and pulled the covers over my head. His pajama top was lying under the covers. It had his scent, and then I wasn't mad anymore. I just felt like wrapping myself up in something that smelled like him. Mark threw back the covers and started pulling me out of bed.

"Come on! Let's go for a ride."

"Where? What for?"

"I need to get out of here. Get up. Get dressed."

"Why do I have to come? You're mad at me. You hate me."

"I love you!" he said angrily. "I feel like dragging you around whether you're dead or alive."

We drove nowhere in particular, stopping to buy orange juice and two gallons of gas. Mark usually managed to obtain gas creds from somewhere, just as I'd always seemed to be able to scrounge up water creds when I needed more water for my plants. We pulled over near a park that was one of the most dangerous areas of the city to walk in. We looked at the dark forms of trees, at the groups of people, at the loners, at the campfires. Mark had some friends who'd been robbed at rifle point on the sidewalk near the park in the middle of the afternoon. I wondered idly whether if I walked across the park now, I could make it unharmed. I fingered the Mace in my pocket. I thought my chances would be fifty-fifty. I asked Mark what he thought.

"Why don't you try it?" he said tiredly.

And the thing was, I had a sudden feeling that it would be sort of exhilarating, sort of really insolent, to try it. It was like when I was a kid and some of us walked along the fourth-floor ledge of a building just for the risk. I felt like going for a walk. I knew it was stupid, but I felt it was also stupidly courageous, and that courage, even stupid courage, was a good antidote not just to fear but to guilt, evil, the anger of someone you loved, and anything else you might need a quick antidote for. I opened the car door and hurried out before I could change my mind. Mark shouted, "What are you doing? I didn't mean it." I could hear his shouting getting closer as he chased after me. He caught up in the park and grabbed me and whipped me around by the arm.

"I said what are you doing?"

"Let go. I'm going for a walk." He shook me once by the arm. "Ouch. Stop it. I'll kick you in the shins if you don't let go."

"I'm serious. What are you doing?"

"I'll kick you."

"If you kick me, I'll kick you back, believe me."

"I'm warning you."

"Likewise."

I kicked him and he didn't kick me back, and then I felt bad that I'd kicked him. We just stood there stupidly for a moment. I heard some men laughing and looked over. One of them shook his head sympathetically to Mark. "You got a wild one there," he said. "I know how that is." Out of his sympathy, safety was born. I saw a rifle lying on the bench next to him, but I knew we were safe.

A couple of police cars, probably just patrolling, started to circle the park, and at the same instant that I saw the cars, three campfires I'd seen before disappeared. There seemed to be fewer people around now, less noise, less movement. The two men nearby looked like stones, very calm, not nervously still but quite still. That's when I had my moment of exhilaration. I felt as if I were in the middle of an invisible city, a Cheshire-cat world where things and people could vanish and appear instantaneously. I stared at the men nearby, at how calm and how still and how almost invisible they were. It just seemed so miraculous and so sad how they could hide from the police without really hiding at all. I don't know why, but I felt somewhat the way I had on the beach with Nadine years earlier. There were certain feelings of camaraderie, and of wistfulness, but the overwhelming feeling was of something ending.

We sat on a bench for a couple of minutes. "So why *are* you so mad?" I said.

"I don't know. I'm not mad at you. I'm just mad."

"You knew we were going to watch Goodman that night. You're the one who dropped me off."

"I know, but when I got home, I started thinking, so I called his home. He was still there. I told him not to go, he said okay, and then I went to sleep."

"Then why did he go anyway? He knew we'd be there."

"It's incomprehensible." He pulled my hand and we walked back to the car. We didn't hold hands warmly, but firmly. He was more pulling me than holding my hand, I guess. We drove back to his place, which was a hothouse since I'd forgotten to turn off the heat when we left. We got in bed and Mark fell right to sleep.

Far away, I heard a helicopter hovering over the city. You heard that noise so frequently you barely noticed it anymore. I sat up to see out the window over the bed. A searchlight was shining down, a mile away. I thought there was probably somebody hiding from that light. I didn't know whether I was on the helicopter's side or on the side of the person it was searching for. I didn't know what was right or wrong. I didn't know anything, except that one man, Goodman, was dead; another man, Rohn, was missing; and another, Burroughs, had possibly killed someone and almost certainly skipped bail. Also, I knew that something was ending, which also meant that something was beginning. But I couldn't say what. I didn't know whether, a hundred years from now, this would be called The Dark Century or The Century of Light. Though others had already declared it the former, I hoped it would turn out to be the latter. I thought the question might be resolved within a decade. I heard the TV from upstairs, as usual. This time it must have been on one of the all-news stations. There'd been a big riot in Houston earlier, in the city's richtown area. I could still remember a time when some people in richtowns spoke out in favor of some of the changes they thought the rioters wanted. Let's have more richtowns, they said. But all pretense of political liberalism among the affluent had evaporated as it became clear that there would be no place for them in a new order. It became clear that the rioters had long ago stopped rioting for change. Now they rioted for destruction. Some people from richtowns were probably quite nice, but after all nobody wanted his or her house burned. Nobody.

"I Was Here"

I saw dead people in the sky. That is, I didn't *see* them, but I knew they were there. They were right behind where the lines of planes flew into the airport. I would look at that section of sky and feel as if my parents were there, and maybe Madeline as well. The clouds and the color of the sky might change, but the people were there, anyway. Sometimes they watched me, but mostly they didn't. There were some people I wished could be alive again, like my parents or certain politicians who'd been assassinated, but there were also people I didn't particularly care about or had never known. They never watched me. I never saw Rohn up there, presumably because he was still alive, and one day I didn't see my parents, either. Eventually no one I knew was there, but others were, watching people I did not know.

Auntie Annie was still writing letters to try to find Rohn. She wrote letters daily, just as she ate and used the bathroom and brushed her teeth daily. It was scary that she was writing those letters, but so far she hadn't gotten in trouble—this, even though she'd written to police and government agencies. Some weeks she went into a frenzy and wrote hundreds of letters. I knew I had to go look for Rohn soon and had decided to make myself as slothful as possible until then. I just wanted to eat tacos and let my fingernails grow and do nothing for a few weeks. I didn't wash my hair for so long you could ice-skate on my greasy head. Finally one day Mark came over acting like a chirp.

"So how's it going?" he said. "So how do you feel? So it's a nice day, huh?"

"It's not going real well, I don't feel so good, and it's incredibly smoggy out."

"What do you mean?" He drew the curtains and I shaded my eyes. "It's great out there." He wrinkled his nose and then got serious. "Listen, no offense, but you're starting to smell. I'll make a deal with you. I'll drive you out to the desert today if you'll just take a shower. And wash your hair with real shampoo, don't just get it wet and spray perfume on it."

"Do I smell?" I said, feeling half pleased, as if I'd accomplished something. I ran my hand through my hair and looked at my palm, shiny now.

"Francie," he said, but he evidently couldn't think of the words to express what he was thinking when he saw my greasy palm.

"I remember when someone down the street lost a relative and all they wrote was one letter to try to find him, and then

they disappeared. So it's better for you if you stay and don't
help me."

"I'll take my chances."

I went to take a shower. The water meter in the hallway
indicated I'd used half as much water this month as I usually
did. I started out with steaming water, then went to lukewarm,
then cool, then back up to lukewarm and steaming again. I
sudsed my face seven times, and scrubbed my body until it
reddened. I scrubbed my skin so hard the black pearls beneath
it fell out and rolled across the tub and down the drain. I ran
a razor over almost my entire body, even over the downy hairs
on my thighs and stomach. I sang. I talked to myself. I imagined.
The water stopped abruptly. I'd used up my household allowance
for the month. To get clean in the coming days, I'd have to use
drinking water, which I had credits for, or one of the pay showers
that had sprung up all over. I never understood why the government had enough water for those businesses, but not enough
for private citizens. It was an hour and a half later, and Mark
had fallen asleep on the couch. I put on a sundress and straw
hat, and put sunscreen and a jacket in a bag with my pouch.

I shook Mark lightly. "What time is it?" he was saying. My
clock was blinking in the dim room. The pocket watch in my
bag said seven o'clock. "Are you ready? You look so clean.
You don't smell," he said lovingly.

"Can we stop at my aunt's apartment?"

"Sure, we'd better hurry, though. I told Carl we'd stop by
and see him. He lives in the desert now."

"The tattooist? Tonight?"

"I said tonight or tomorrow. He knows a lot of people out
there. He might be able to help us."

I called Auntie, but she wasn't home, so I told her machine where Mark and I were going. Mark already had his bag
in the car.

"How did you know we'd be going tonight?" I said. "How'd you know I'd agree?"

"I saw it in a dream," he said happily, though he never remembered his dreams. He was just teasing me for being superstitious all the time.

The weather was uncommonly cold in the upper elevations. It was actually snowing in some parts, everything pink, gray, and black. Sometimes we could barely see out the windows, the snow-hail falling with pings on the roof. The sky was black between the clouds. Giant forms we could barely make out lurked on both sides of the highway at one point. Along many freeways in Southern California, huge steel and paper-mâché animals, people, cartoon characters, or *things* had been built to entice people to stop at restaurants, gift shops, or gas stations. One place had built dinosaurs; another, further north, had a thermometer sixty feet tall. Both those had been built before the turn of the century. Visibility was so low it wasn't safe to drive, so we pulled over and parked next to a monstrous hand with a teacup on the tip of one of its fingers. We were in the carnival town of Darcy, named for the man who started it as a cult colony about fifty years earlier. The cult had gone out of business, and now the town barely made a living from people driving by, on the way from one place to another. There were a few carnival rides. We'd parked not far from one—teacups that would twirl around and around, even, if we desired, now, out in the cold and snow. There was also an oil-wrestling arena, where you paid to wrestle with naked men or women. You were supposed to cover yourself with cooking oil and wrestle with the person or persons of your choice. The lights by the teacups were on and there was an "Open" sign, but no one was around. We rang a bell and presently a boy about our age came out.

"Can we ride?" said Mark.

"Yeh," the boy said. He pointed to the "We never close"

that was scrawled on the "Open" sign. He walked over to a crank and pushed it. The teacups shivered and squeaked. "It's gotta warm up. That'll be fifty cents apiece." You couldn't buy anything for fifty cents anymore, but probably nobody would ride the teacups if they cost more. Mark handed him two dollars and we got into the cups under the falling snow. "Don't stop in the middle," said Mark. "Just let it keep going for the two rides' worth."

The snow whipped against my cheeks, and I needed to close my eyes against it. When I squinted, all I saw were dim lights, dark forms, and snatches of color. The other teacups swirled around us, their colors muted by the snow, and the wind snuck up the sleeves of my jacket. The only part of me that was entirely warm was the part pressing against Mark. I couldn't tell whether thirty seconds or three minutes had passed, but finally the teacups stopped. It took a second to get oriented. The snow had let up a bit, making it seem as if the world had somehow altered while we were spinning. When we got out, we ran in the building nearby to warm up.

We were in a foyer with plants painted on the walls; in front of the paintings, a fake dracaena in a pot reached for the low ceiling. We leaned close together as we tried to get our insides warm again. The boy came in. "I can get you a cup of hot water for a quarter."

"Do you have any herbs?" I asked.

He shook his head no, so we paid him a quarter for the water. He disappeared into a back room. As he slipped through the door, I saw two infants and a girl about my age inside. A sign outside had said there was a palm reader here. It was probably the girl. The boy brought the water out and watched impassively as Mark and I took turns sipping.

"Gonna ride again?"

"No, I don't think so," said Mark.

He watched us with a gaze that was ninety-eight percent bored and two percent interested. The two percent part said, "Delivery business?"

Mark nodded yes and handed him the cup. "Thanks," Mark said, but the boy had already turned around and headed into the back room.

Since the snow had let up, we resumed our drive to the motel where Auntie and I used to stay with Rohn. We passed a toxic waste dump to the south and didn't talk much as we passed. Something about it always made me not feel like talking, as if it might hurt someone if not shown the proper respect. The town the motel was in was dark. It seemed dead, not asleep, and the lights didn't work inside the cold room Auntie and I still kept the keys to. Mark shined a flashlight around and we got under the covers to keep warm. We made love between the scratchy sheets as the power returned and the clock began blinking in the darkness. Afterward, we ate some freeze-dried chicken we'd brought, then we got dressed and went back outside.

"Everybody must be asleep," I whispered.

The trucks were driving across the way, in the cold, cold light of the power plant and industrial town beyond. I had a blanket wrapped around me.

"Let's go over there and see what's going on," said Mark. We started walking across the dark field, but it seemed that no matter how much we walked we didn't get any nearer. It was like walking toward the moon to try to get closer. Finally we returned to our car. We drove around searching for a road perpendicular to the one the trucks drove on, but there didn't seem to be any. We decided to drive across the field. With every bump our heads hit the roof of the car, even with our restraints on. The ride was much longer than it had appeared. And then when we finally arrived we didn't know what to do next. We turned off the engine and watched the trucks, same as we'd been doing on the other side, except now we were closer. Most of the drivers ignored us, but now and then someone looked down, mildly surprised. We were freezing, since we didn't have a car heater. The trucks rumbled along. Mark suddenly turned on the engine, and, at a small break in the traffic, we hurtled across the road. There was a small office near the power plant. No one answered when we knocked, so we fell into line on the road.

"It's weird," I said. "I feel like if we could just figure out what was going on here, we could find Rohn, or figure out where he is, or figure out *something*."

"I feel like if we could find out what was going on," said Mark, "we would have figured out one piece of a puzzle. But then there would be another piece after that."

We drove for a couple of hours. It was already getting light, barely. We pulled over to a gas station where a few trucks were parked. We were the only car. The drivers looked at us curiously. One of them, an amiable man with skin almost as red as it was brown, approached us.

"Lost?" he said, smiling.

"Actually, we're looking for somebody," I said before Mark could stop me. As long as we were here, it made sense to take at least a few chances and trust somebody.

The man's eyes glazed over and he nodded his head to signal that we should move farther away from where the other drivers stood. He moved with us. "You'd better turn back."

"Where does this road lead to?" I asked.

"Some warehouses."

"Whose warehouses?" I could see the sun peeking up behind the man.

He studied his cup of coffee. "They're Uncle Sam's." He raised his eyes to us. "It's nothing important. I'm delivering desks, myself. I take the desks over to the warehouse and when someone needs them I take the desks back from the warehouse. I don't know what all those other trucks are carrying."

"I thought once about getting a driving job," said Mark.

"It's a good job. It pays well." The man furrowed his brows, much the way Mark sometimes did. "How old are you kids?"

"Nineteen."

"You don't look it, but then I'm getting old. Everybody looks young to me." He shook his head at us, as if amazed at the stupidity of youth, and then he swept his arm toward the horizon. "Did you know that every square mile in this country is owned by someone, and the owner's name is recorded on a computer somewhere? They say the highways are public, but public means owned by the government as far as I'm concerned." He leaned closer. "I only drive as far as they tell me to drive. I don't drive past that. But I've heard that some of the truckers carry prisoners. I've heard there are prisons out there, past where I drive to. Prisons like warehouses."

"How far?" said Mark.

"*Far*. It's all government land. They won't sell you gas along the way. What kind of weapons do you have?" he demanded. "Whatever you have, it's not enough."

"Well, we didn't plan on having to use them," I said. I felt the familiar weight of my Mace in my pocket. But it didn't comfort me the way it usually did. It felt like a toy. I looked hopefully down the road.

"Forget it. It's suicide," said the man. "Heaven's not everything it's cracked up to be. Stick around." He saw someone in a uniform walking toward us and he turned and hurried away toward the uniformed man. "Just kids. They're lost. They were having a joy ride."

We got back in our car and turned around, driving back to the field we'd crossed. Mark pointed out some graffiti on the side of an outhouse near the power plant: AAA. That stood for the Anti-Aryan Association, a fringe group with what authorities estimated was "not more than a hundred members." At least, that's what the papers always said. I'd never met a member, just seen the graffiti. The huge red A's must have been fairly recent or someone would have removed them by now. I wondered what the AAA had been doing in an industrial no-town like this.

We took a nap at the motel and in the afternoon went to visit Carl. Mark had called him when we returned from the truckers' road. Carl, who'd cut down his workload to one tattoo a day, raised chickens and cacti now, and also sold books, still cameras, and other old-fashioned but popular items. He lived about twenty miles away.

"Did you tell him why we were coming?" I asked.

"Nope, not outright anyway. I hinted."

Before we'd reached the top steps leading to Carl's plain white house, he opened the door. "Eggs!" he exclaimed. "I've got the best layers in the state. We're having eggs for lunch. Omelettes."

"Unprocessed food?" I said. Carl winked at me and I smiled. "It smells great in here. You've already started cooking."

"I started because I knew you wouldn't be late. I knew you were the kind of girl who's never late."

"That's news to me," said Mark.

Carl had set the table with some pretty homemade pottery. "A friend of mine made these. I designed them."

Black spiked tattoos stuck up from the neckholes of his shirt. I hadn't noticed them before, but maybe this shirt revealed more than the last one I'd seen him wearing. Tattoos were just starting to move quickly out of trendiness, at least for the vast numbers of people who were neither insiders nor outsiders. Now it was often either outsiders or insiders who made up his clientele. Cops or criminals, the very rich or the very poor. Carl was like a priest. As he drew with his needle on people's skin, they told him their secrets. As a professional, he never told who'd told him what, but maybe for Mark he would make an exception.

While Carl was readying lunch, I leafed through his portfolio, which had been sitting on a bookshelf. He specialized in stark, mostly black and gold designs. In fact, he was the foremost practitioner of that style of tattoo on the West Coast. There was one picture of a man whose face and bald head were striped black.

"I thought he didn't do faces," I said.

Mark peered over my shoulder. "He doesn't as far as I know."

"Lunch is on!"

"I thought you didn't do faces," I said. I held up the picture to him.

"I did his shoulders. I never do faces."

"Is that a rule?"

"That's a rule."

"Is there an exception to the rule?" I asked.

"If there's an exception, it's not a rule."

The man's shoulders were a sunburst of black, red, gold, and blue. Silver, gold, and other metallics were extremely popular in tattoos today. "I can't get used to tattooing like this on people's faces."

"So what?" said Carl. "That's fine to say, but where do you go from there? What do you do with that? It's not against the law to make yourself ugly in the eyes of the majority. It's not against the Constitution, although some people seem to think it is."

"No," I said. "It's not. Why don't you do faces?"

"Because when someone comes to me and says he or she wants a face tattoo, I say they don't know whether they do or not, since they've never had one. How do they know they want one? They don't know what it's like to be ugly in the eyes of the majority."

The omelettes were fantastic, not at all like the gunk I ordinarily ate. We also drank red wine that a friend of Carl's had made. I admired and envied his self-sufficiency. He even had a huge tank filled with emergency water. It was illegal to hoard water, even if you'd obtained it legally. He told us that that was the only law he broke, not because he believed in the laws but because he was practical. If he broke the laws, he might get arrested, and if he got arrested he wouldn't be self-sufficient any longer. His independence was more important to him than anything.

"But one thing I've learned is that they like you to break laws," he said. "They like to have something on you. So I knew they wouldn't mind if I got the tank, if they ever knew I'd got one. They, they, they. I don't want to talk about them."

"So do you get a lot of work out here?" said Mark.

"Pretty good, things are pretty good. I'm not working much now. I don't feel like it. It's funny. I remember when I started I was desperate to find people to tattoo. It was a hunger like the hunger for our most basic needs. I used to work on people who didn't matter, and when I say they didn't matter, I mean it didn't matter to them if they got a tattoo or not. I'd give someone a beer and practice tattooing them. Then, when I got a little better I'd give away free tattoos, no beer. Then cheap tattoos, and finally people were coming to me. And now here I am, half the time I don't feel like working."

We ate in silence for a moment. Mark raised his eyebrows at me. "We're searching for someone," he said. "A friend of Francie's is missing. The last time she saw him wasn't far from here, at that old ghost town."

Carl continued to eat. He downed his fourth glass of wine and poured another. He'd told us earlier in the morning that we could come by for either lunch or dinner, but that during the afternoon he was more likely to be sober, unless, as today, he didn't have any clients. "Who is this that's missing?" Carl finally asked.

"Sort of her surrogate father. He lived with her aunt and helped raise her."

"They took me in when I was thirteen and my parents died. His name is Rohn."

"Last name?"

"Jefferson."

"How did he disappear?"

I told him about the water deal.

"Do you know Max the Magician?" said Mark.

Carl nodded yes. "But I don't know a lot about him. He's around and he's been around for a long time. I know other things, too, but I've never dealt with him in any way."

"We have to find him," I said. "We have to find Max and we have to find Rohn."

"Why do you *have* to find Rohn?"

"Because my aunt loves him."

Carl laughed. "Love . . . love . . . I may be able to help. It may take awhile, though. I'll ask around." He chuckled briefly again.

"We don't want it to drag on too long," said Mark. "Who knows what's happening to him? It's no good for us if we find him running around waving a hatchet at the sun and talking to himself."

"That would be better than nothing," I said.

"That would be worse than nothing," said Mark.

Carl looked thoughtful. "Good, good," he said to me. "Because your aunt loves him. That's a good answer." His retriever entered from a side door and Carl threw him a piece of bread without looking at him.

After lunch Mark and I cleared the dishes while Carl stayed at the table with his wine. We went to wash dishes in the kitchen.

"Don't use a lot of water!" Carl shouted to us.

"What do you think?" I said quietly to Mark.

"He'll do what he can. He's a good man. In fact, I hope he doesn't try to do too much and get in trouble, but I'm sure he's too smart for that."

There was a Japanese word that my mother had taught me before she died: *yoyu,* and although it didn't translate exactly, it meant somewhere between "enough" and "abundance." It meant "something left over," a spiritual excess that allowed some people to be generous. Carl possessed *yoyu.*

The kitchen window was open despite the chilliness. Chickens clucked among the cacti in the back yard. "Do you think he gets lonely out here?"

"Sure."

"Why do you think he stays, then?"

"I don't know. Whenever anyone states an opinion, he always asks, 'That's fine, but what do you do with that?' If you asked him whether he was lonely, he would say, 'Okay, but what do you do with that?' That doesn't mean I don't think he's happy, because I think he is. He was a great tattooist. People came to him from all over the world. That gives him a lot of satisfaction. He wasn't always the best, but he was always real good. Maybe, for a few months or years, he was considered the best. When you think that only one person at a time can be the best, that's quite an achievement."

Carl entered, sat at the kitchen table, and opened another wine bottle.

"You should come into the city sometimes and visit with us," I said. "It's lonesome out here."

"What makes you think it's less lonesome in the city?" We'd finished cleaning up and sat at the kitchen table with him.

"There's so much space in this house. Everywhere you look in the desert there's space. It makes me uncomfortable."

"No one knows how to feel today," Carl said. Mark and I waited for him to explain. "When I was starting out as a tattooist, I'd be pressing the needle into someone's skin. I didn't know what I was doing. You'd think giving someone a tattoo is a visual act, but it's not, strictly speaking. It's like when you cut a tomato with a new knife you've never used, or with somebody else's knife. You're not exactly sure how hard to press at first, although you have a pretty good idea, because you know something about knives and you know something about tomatoes. But I didn't know anything about skin. There were no reference points for me. What I learned right away was that when I made mistakes, I always made them on the side of not pressing hard enough, so the tattoo ended up too pale. That's a common mistake for beginners, and it's not the end of the world. I would just bull the person, tell him or her that their skin was especially tough, come back again and I'll work on it some more. I learned how much power I had. Another thing I had to think about was hurting the person. Maybe that bothered me once or twice, but I got over that real quick. Pain is just a concomitant to getting a tattoo. It hurts, but so what? So I learned what to feel about hurting people." He finished a glass of wine and drank straight from the bottle now.

Mark said, "Hey, it's none of my business, but maybe it's too early for this." He nodded at the wine bottle.

"We're having a philosophical discussion here," said Carl. "Do you mind? Where was I? Is anybody listening?"

"You were talking about hurting people," Mark said resignedly.

"Sometimes a customer comes in and wants me to do something that can't be done properly, say, an impressionistic painting. I'll tell them it's not possible, nobody can do it. They try to manipulate me with mindless flattery and overstatement of my qualifications. And that's boring. So that's how I feel about that.

"Sometimes people think there's something magical about tattooing. That's fine with me. It's good for business. It helps keep customers in line if they think you're a voodoo artist. But that's not me.

"Sometimes someone has almost all of his body tattooed. I've never started anyone with his first tattoo who later became covered with tattoos, and I've never done the last. I was always in the middle. Sometimes they'll come back to me repeatedly, filling up their skin. And I tell them to slow down, that bare skin is money in the bank. But they want a tattoo. So I accept that. It's not my business.

"What I'm saying is, I've learned to know how I feel about most things. I've learned how hard to press, I've learned what I think about various types of flattery and lies and illusions. I've learned to accept and reject." He turned to me and rose up in his chair. "So don't treat me like some poor little lonely boy out in the big bad desert who you need to invite to dinner. I know just how I felt about being in Los Angeles, I know just how I feel about being here, and I know just how I feel about you."

I picked up a white dishrag and waved it. "I surrender."

Carl sat back in his chair and after a moment he winked at Mark.

"So have you ever talked to Max the Magician?" I said. "He seems omnipotent to me."

Carl sighed. "I guess we're not going to have any nice after-meal conversation." He looked at Mark. "Are we?"

"She's a pitiless machine sometimes," he said.

Carl sighed again. "Max is not magic. That's the first thing you need to know about Max. He doesn't know everything, he can't do everything. He knows magic. That's it. And he always needs money. Those are the only two things you need to know about him."

"How much money might he need?"

"Who can say? I'll put out some feelers. Come back tomorrow. Now, if it's all the same to you, I think I'll retire." His head clunked down on the table and in a second he was snoring.

Mark and I placed a cushion from the living room under his head and let ourselves out.

"Shall we stop at the ghost town?" I said.

"Might as well."

We stopped off there but found nothing. Nothing at all had changed, except that the last time I'd been here, Rohn's smell had still hung in the air. Now the air smelled clean, not at all like the exhaust-filled smells of the city.

"I wonder whether people really lived here once," I said.

"I think they did. Hey, did you know there's an old cemetery around here? Lucas said he's been out this way."

"Shall we search over there? I mean if they, um, if he—I mean, I'm sure he's still alive."

"We can go take a look, but no messing around with the dead and none of your superstitious business when we get there. The last thing I need is a bunch of ghosts on my tail."

I couldn't tell if he was kidding or not. The cemetery, only thirty or forty graves, had been rifled, and what remained were weeds, mounds of dirt, fallen and broken stones. We paused at the threshold to the cemetery, under a gateway that still stood, though it was no longer necessary since most of the walls around the grounds had fallen or been broken through. It was typical of an unguarded cemetery.

"He's not here," I said. "I know it." Mark looked at me. "I *know* it."

We returned to the motel. We had only one gas cred left, for five gallons, and we were low on gas, so we hung around the motel. All afternoon and evening, we played gin rummy. That night when I closed my eyes I saw hearts, clubs, diamonds, and spades. I saw diamond lights, blue hearts, clubs growing on stems, and faces shaped like spades. All night during my dreams, images of cards popped up, rolled by, or fell from the sky. Hearts rained down during a storm, and a gun shot black diamonds for bullets. Club-shaped ashes flew from a fire.

The next morning we drove back to Carl's. It was much warmer today, but with a hard wind. Everything around us, the trees and cacti and occasional houses, seemed to be succumbing to the wind, not as if the wind were pushing them but as if it were pulling and sucking at them. When the wind blew I felt as if something were trying to suck us off the road.

When we arrived at Carl's, he came out of his house and talked to us by the car. "I've got a client in there."

"Thanks for taking the time," said Mark.

"Sure, it's fine. She's driving me crazy. A long time ago I had a woman who insisted I do her an ear tattoo. It's a pain in the ass to do ears and I don't like the way they come out, so I said no. She insisted. I had to call the police to get her out of my shop. This lady must be her sister—she wants a rose on the side of her nose."

The shades of his house were pulled down but they rustled for a moment.

"What did you find out?" said Mark.

"I've heard they've been making more arrests than they can handle and they're going to be releasing some people in the next few months. So maybe her aunt's friend will be among those released. As for Max, he's moved up north about fifty miles. I doubt he knows anything."

"We heard there might be a prison further east."

"Really? I've never heard that. But so what? What are you going to do, break him out?"

The door to his house opened. "Are you going to do it or not?" said the woman inside. She had her hair in a long black and white-blond braid, and her lips were intensely red.

"I've got to go. I'll let you know if I hear more." He walked in a leisurely fashion up to the house. At the door he turned around and said, "Go home," and then he went inside. We could hear muffled sounds of the woman yelling at him from behind the door.

"What do you think?" Mark said.

"I guess that's all we can do, unless we go to the jail. But that doesn't seem advisable."

We'd already packed our things and started the drive back directly from Carl's. Mark slept beside me. I stopped at a gas station and used up our last gas credit. Nobody was working at the station, so I just pushed the credit into a slot over the pump. Dust whirled upward at the horizon as the pump burped out a receipt. All around me old receipts rustled over the asphalt. The garbage can was overflowing. I picked up a few receipts to read their dates. The most recent was from two weeks earlier. I wrote "I was here" on the back of mine and let it fly toward the dust-filled sky as I drove off.

Helicopters

A cloud landed one day on top of the tallest building in Los Angeles, the Natsumi Hotel. The hotel, built by one of the wealthiest women in Japan and named for her daughter, was the source of considerable controversy when it opened two decades earlier. *Natsumi* means "summer." Twenty years ago, hatred of Japan was so fierce that the City Council actually debated whether they could force the hotel to be called the Summer Hotel. But reason prevailed and it was called Natsumi. Rich summer colors circled the top of the building—green, turquoise, magenta, gold, and lavender. The cloud settled on top of these colors as if the hotel were a magnet and the cloud, iron filings.

That same day, there were seven thousand arrests in Los Angeles. It was the day of the June primary, and for the first time in years, turnout was high. There were no extraordinary measures on the ballot, nor were there any extraordinary candidates. Everyone just sort of went wild and voted. A friend of mine from a geology class I'd taken was arrested for trying to keep his ballot, which he'd voted on but refused to place in the ballot box. He told me he'd just wanted to see whether the ballot belonged to him or to the government. Others were arrested at protests against all the various parties, and fights broke out in a number of precincts. Everybody was feeling rambunctious. A store clerk was rude to me, and I considered spitting at her, but didn't. But I did refuse to buy my groceries even though she'd already packed them. And then I yelled at and shook my Mace gun at several drivers during the day. I saw three different people indulge in the newest fad among irate drivers—shooting paint at cars that had cut them off on the freeway.

The winds that finally blew away the clouds were hard, dry, and warm, and they left the sky blue. As if they'd bloomed overnight, yellow gazanias covered a section of one of the Hollywood Hills, the yellow stunning against the sky. That section of the hill was No Trespass, government owned, and apparently someone had planted the gazanias as a friendly protest of sorts against the government. After the winds, a calm settled over the city, and it was the calm that ironically made me feel that the end of calm was fast approaching. By the third day of the winds, the city was starting to seem battered. Fronds of wind-burnt palms lay in all the roads, and toppled plastic trees lay across lawns and sidewalks.

A long time ago, Rohn had bought some land in the desert, in godforsaken country where nobody lived. He'd built a shelter in the ground, and Mark and I decided to take our most precious things, as well as the most important possessions of our friends, to the shelter. My most important possessions at one time had been my plants, and I didn't really have anything now, but I took some things for Annie. Rohn had said that he would be able to get gas and water in an emergency. "I have connections you'd best not know about," he had told me. Even with the water pipeline from Alaska finally operational—they'd been building it since the nineties—the state was one of the dryest in the country because of a combination of drought and over-population.

Since childhood, I'd fantasized about finding a town my friends and I could live in, safely and happily. Now I saw there would be no town, but we did have half an acre of barren land to give sanctuary to our possessions.

There was other business to take care of. After we returned from the possessions shelter, I went downtown to renew my aunt's delivery license. Usually you could do this by mail, but this year they'd said somebody had to come in person, maybe to punish Auntie for all the letters she'd been writing about Rohn. She was always busy running the business—she had a couple of employees now—so I went downtown for her. Unfortunately, the buses were on strike and I needed to drive. There was one block that took me fifteen minutes to get down because traffic was so heavy. In richtown, marquees were all in English, except when a European film was playing at an art film house. Downtown, writing on the marquees was all in either Spanish or Korean. The streets were lined with small swap shops, and the Grand Central Public Market was crowded with food vendors. The smell of fish wafted into the car. I bought a couple of shriveled mangoes from a man walking up and down the streets between the trapped cars. Nearby, a boy grabbed a handful of grapes—probably moldy—from a fruit seller and tore off down the crowded sidewalk, dodging and pushing people as he ran. Impressed by his speed and daring, everyone laughed while the fruit seller swore.

Finally, I was able to pull into the Dungeon, formally known as The Downtown Los Angeles Memorial Parking Facility. The lights inside were so faded I needed to keep my headlamps on. A lot of city workers parked here, and the upper levels were filled. I didn't find a space until Level Seven Down.

When I got out I heard a clanking and whirring that I supposed came from air vents, but the air was so stale it was hard to believe it was being ventilated at all. There was a purplish pall cast by the lights. You couldn't see the whole eight-block length of the lot. Sections were cut off from each other, creating a maze effect, and the maps to guide you were often faded or covered with political posters: REVOLT or DON'T VOTE or VOTE. At least if the rooms weren't cut off from each other, you could expect to see someone once in a while, but sectioned off as it was, the place often made you feel as if you were the only person down there. Some sections stretched on for longer than others, but my section was cut off from the rest of the lot. There seemed to be no rhyme or reason for it all. Most of the people who parked at the lower levels probably had business at one of the nearby government buildings: Criminal Courts, Small Claims, County Recorder, the new Licensing and Permit Building, the Federal Courthouse. On and on. I heard a car alarm bleep briefly and my heart skipped a beat because the sound of that mechanical voice signaled the existence of a person who must have set it off.

The elevator took forever. When I got upstairs, I faced a long line for licensing papers. The line handled both delivery and vending licenses, so there were a lot of people. I had to quell the feelings of bondage that always rose in me when I was waiting in a long line. I took a brochure from a rack. The brochure, called "Making City Government Work for You," pictured a smiling middle-class couple on the cover. I couldn't imagine what they were smiling about, unless it was because they never had to come downtown to face these lines. The woman at the front of my line was having a quiet but furious argument with the clerk. Behind me, someone smelled bad. The woman before me had brought her three children. I looked longingly at the door behind me. I looked longingly at the front of the line. One of the woman's children was pointing at her crying brother and saying to her mother, "I didn't hit him, I didn't kick him, I didn't pull his hair." Her mother smacked her on the side of the head anyway, and the boy stuck out his tongue ever-so-slightly at his sister. I read my whole brochure, then I perused a sheet from some classified ads that had been lying on the floor. Standing captive in that line, I felt susceptible to the classifieds. I wanted to go out and buy a red divan or find some child's lost Dalmatian. I'd read an entire page of want ads and had just started the other side when I reached the front of the line.

The clerk didn't lift her head so I said, "I need to renew a delivery license."

"Uh-huh," she said, still without looking up. She turned and walked away to a file cabinet a few windows down, and after searching for a while, she spoke a few words to another clerk before returning to look over my papers.

"Four hundred dollars," she said.

I handed her the money and she counted it expertly. She stamped my papers, handed me one of the stamped sheets, and said, "They'll send the license in the mail."

I was glad to be finished with the line, but I would be gladder when I was out of that parking lot. The elevator never came, so I walked down the stairs, passing a couple of police with a handcuffed man, and three men in suits. There was a man lounging near a car in my section of Level Seven, and I gripped my Mace and filled my heart with hate. But it was nothing, so I got in my car, letting the hate evaporate, and drove the seven levels up. I felt relieved to see the dirty sky and the crowded street. It seemed fresh and beautiful in a way it rarely did. The existence of light and life seemed to me a godsend.

When I arrived home, Mark was there taping up my windows. Helicopters were planning to spray the entire city that night with Benfarzine, a new insecticide developed to stop a seemingly unstoppable fruit fly that had invaded the state. Despite the constant drought, agriculture was still vitally important to California. Since more and more businesses had chosen to locate elsewhere because of low water supplies and crowded, polluted conditions, agriculture had taken a place of absolute eminence.

Mark and I turned off the lights and sat in chairs we pulled up to a window. We filled cups with iced tea and waited for sundown and the arrival of the copters. He saw them first. "There!" he said. Two lines of six copters each were moving through the sky. The spray they were dropping was a vague mist. They flew slowly back and forth, sometimes moving out of our vision and then returning slightly closer. Other formations of helicopters were doing other sections of the city. I had never seen the city so still. Employers had been asked to stagger the times when workers could go home, to prevent traffic jams as everyone tried to make it to their homes before the spraying started. Mark and I were silent for a long time, but once, when the copters made a reappearance, we instinctively reached for each other's hand.

We could hear my next-door neighbors fighting. The woman was crying and shouting, "I hate you! I hate you!" A lone car hurried through a red light. Mark and I had purchased a great deal of food and water for the occasion, as if we were stuck in here for days rather than overnight. All of a sudden the helicopters emerged much closer than I'd expected, and I realized it was another group, coming from the opposite direction. They seemed to have appeared from another dimension. On the next run, the noise was deafening, and I could feel my insides shaking. White spray fell through the air outside, blurring the view. I leaned back from the window. The whole sky was lit up by the lights from the helicopters. I couldn't help getting a thrill from the sheer seductive power of the noise and speed. Pesticides and mysticism, police and religion—people were always looking for powerful forces to change the world, or to help conquer other forces.

The helicopters near us moved away, but I could see others in the distance. In the temporary quiet, I felt as if the world was falling apart, and the feeling didn't go away during the next pass, or the next, or the next. Finally there was silence, and then suddenly we could hear the woman who'd been crying laughing hysterically. Someone seemed to be tickling her. Mark and I had to smile at her hysterical laughter. The whole city had just been bugbombed, but I couldn't help feeling hopeful.

To me, love and hate were not the opposites. Love and pain were. It was not hate, but pain, that love assuaged, opposed, canceled out.

Mark turned on the lights so we could start cooking dinner.

"I notice you bought some new plants," he said.

"I saw them sitting in a store and I decided to liberate them."

He laughed. "You live in a wacky world there in your head, don't you?"

We stood one more moment at the window. Next door was silent. The whole city was silent. Two lines of six lights flew, far away. Besides the fruit flies, other insects had probably also been harmed from the spray. I thought of all the life out there that was now dying. I am not saying that I felt sympathetic or empathetic with all those bugs, just that the thought of a million creatures dying at once amazed me as much as anything ever had.

In the Valley of Love

When I was a child, my friends and I used to play what we called the fainting game. One of us at a time would breathe hard until we felt dizzy, and then someone else would wrap his arms around you and squeeze until you fainted. While you were unconscious, you had vivid dreams, somehow unlike the dreams of sleep. The next time you opened your eyes you were lying on your back, and all your friends were leaning over you saying, "What did you see? What did you see?"

I struggled to tell everything I'd seen before it slipped away. "There was a cat, and a garage, and"— I was already forgetting—"and a long hallway." One

by one, each of us would faint, and then we all sat around trying
to evaluate our dreams. It was as if we had to know something,
but we didn't know what it was we had to know. And we were
so desperate, we thought these dreams would tell us. Later, we'd
go back to more normal games—tag or leapfrog—and we'd
play in the soft wind as late into the night as our parents would
let us.

I think that sense of having to know something elusive was
why Jewel wanted to find out the reason her grandfather had
taken Hank to a secluded spot in the Pasadena Arroyo. Rioting
was spreading like wildfire across the country, but before Jewel
could decide what to do next with her life, she had to know
what was in the arroyo. She seemed to think she couldn't make
a reasonable decision without finding out her grandfather's secret. The chances that we could find the same place seemed
pretty slender to me, yet it didn't seem impossible. Mark, Lucas,
and I accompanied her.

The arroyo was miles long, a valley once filled with trees
and walking paths and surrounded on both sides by pastoral
Pasadena homes. Now somebody—no one was sure who—was
dumping garbage into the arroyo. And it was unsafe to walk in
after dusk. Nowhere was exactly safe anymore.

We brought our guns—I with Mace and the other three
with real guns—and began walking in the morning. Nowhere
did we find the house on the cliff with a wall of windows,
but every so often we searched secluded areas. We stopped
in early afternoon for lunch in one of those areas, setting up
a radio on a fallen tree. Riots. Riots. Riots. We turned the
radio off. All the trees in the arroyo were real, but most
were dried out. Fires had become more common than they
used to be, and we passed a couple of places where the
ravine's growth had burned in the past, black-edged stumps

sticking up from the dirt. We ate bread and canned fish. I was getting blisters on my hands from digging with the shovels we'd brought.

"So what are you guys going to do?" said Jewel. She meant were we planning to stay in the city or leave.

"Staying," we said. Lucas said he was staying as well.

"Why?" she said.

"It's my home," he said.

"What is your aunt doing?" she asked me.

"She's moving into the house we used to live in and waiting for Rohn."

"She's heard from him?"

"No, but she will. I know it." I was certain. The government couldn't be bothered with petty criminals like him anymore. After all, we were all petty criminals in one way or another. I was so certain Rohn would return that my worry now was not whether he could come back, but what he would be like and how he had changed.

Jewel turned to Mark. "Where do your folks live? You never say anything about them." She started coughing and Mark had to wait to speak.

"In Washington. I never see them."

"Why not?"

"Because I don't like them."

Jewel turned to me and mouthed the word "oh." She began coughing again, this time for longer, and I think all of us at once, even her, realized that she was really sick. I felt scared but not surprised. "I'm *fine*," she said firmly, though no one had asked her anything.

It was midafternoon when we reached the end of the arroyo, and we hadn't found anything. We took the sidewalk outside the arroyo on the way back, making much better time on our return trip. We'd started our drive back into town when Lucas said, "I know where it is."

Jewel braked so hard we all jerked forward and the car screeched. "Where?" she said.

"Somewhere around the middle. It's not windows. I just figured it out. It's solar panels, but he just thought they were windows. I remember looking up once and seeing a line of panels that, when I think about it now, could have been mistaken for windows, or misremembered as windows."

We parked the car again and walked down the ravine. The sun was already starting to set. As soon as we reached bottom, we saw several gun-toting boys in the distance, and we hid behind some trees as they passed. We didn't want a confrontation. We stood like statues, lightly touching each other.

"Hey, man, I do what I do," one of the boys was saying as they passed. "I keep my accounts paid up."

When they were out of sight, we set off again.

"There it is!" I said. The panels were set at an angle more vertical than usual. Trees made it hard to see the house below, so the panels took on the appearance of slanted windows if you looked at them right.

"We've already searched here," said Jewel.

"We'll do a better job this time," I said.

Behind some trees, cut off from the rest of the arroyo, we began to search again. Some of the dirt was already soft from where we'd dug earlier. After a while Mark squinted up at the sky. "We should have brought a flashlight."

"Got it!" said Lucas. He hit his shovel on something hard in the ground.

"It's bones I'll bet," said Jewel. "I bet he killed someone."

"It's a box of some sort," said Lucas. We were all kneeling down now and moving dirt with our hands. After a moment we lifted out an old metal cash box wrapped in plastic. I rammed the end of a shovel into the decrepit lock, and it went flying easily off.

Jewel grabbed the box. We squatted around as she opened it. Inside were a couple of old photographs that we could no longer quite make out but that seemed to be of a man and a woman. On the back of one, some writing was scribbled. There seemed to be a date—1998. There were also two gold rings in the box. One was inscribed "To Hank"—Hank was her grandfather's as well as her father's name—and the other said "To Maria."

"Was Maria your grandmother?" I said.

She shook her head no. "She was my great-aunt."

"He loved your great-aunt?"

"He used to love his wife, but she didn't love him."

"How did they end up married?"

Jewel turned irritably away. "She was poor, and he made a lot of money at the time."

"I wonder who Maria loved," I said.

"She never married."

We all sat there, filling in details in our heads about what we thought it all meant.

"I don't know," said Jewel. "I thought he killed someone. I'm kind of disappointed." She picked up the rings and turned them over in her hand. Her disappointed face transformed as she gazed at the rings. It was as if she held love there in her outstretched palm, if love could be held physically.

We decided to rebury everything, so Jewel dropped the rings back into the box. They clinked against the metal, and then we shoveled dirt over the box and threw some debris over the whole thing. We sat quietly in the clearing. It was getting dark. I didn't know what everyone else was thinking about. I was examining

my blisters, and thinking of her grandfather, in love with someone named Maria but never leaving his wife. We heard a rustling,
and a possum hurried through the clearing. It was pleasantly
cool out, and I loved the sound of real leaves hitting each other
all around me.

And there, in the heart of the arroyo on a warm evening in
June, was the last time the four of us were ever in the same
place at the same time. The next day Jewel decided that the
only way she could get herself away from Teddy was to move,
and she wanted to go out east where she had an old friend. Her
decision was totally unexpected. I'd come to expect that she
was glued to Teddy. When she called me and said she was
going, at first I thought she just wanted me to say, "No, stay in
Los Angeles." Often, she called you up only to test you, to make
sure you were still there for her.

"There's only two choices," she said. "Leaving or staying.
And I can't stay."

On the day her plane took off, there was a huge black arc
of smoke across the sky, from an out-of-control fire an arsonist
had set. Mark and I watched her plane rise above the arc. That
night, President Connors made a speech about the country's
problems. So many people were listening to or watching him
that I could hear his voice not from any specific place but from
all around me. The air itself seemed to be speaking. "Some
people have no respect for property," he said, hitting one fist
into another. "And the good people of this nation will not tolerate
that." His words reminded me of one of those car alarms everyone had that said, "You're touching private property. Please
stand away" or "I'm going to call the police" or "Help!"

Mark and I decided that I should give up my apartment and
move into his place. I'd begun to accumulate more plants
again—too many for his small place—so I decided to return
what I had to the nursery where I'd sold my plants before. But

when I went there, the nursery was gone, the bamboo fence removed and the trees cut down. That made me feel like the moment before you cry, the moment before an explosion of tears. I didn't cry, though, just kept feeling like that moment-before all day. I felt very scared as well.

Time seemed to have accelerated. I tried to slow it down by concentrating on each little thing in my path, but it was far beyond my power. I received a letter from Jewel a few weeks after the postmark said she'd sent it. It was a long letter, and she rambled, about the day in the arroyo, about her parents, about school and how much she'd liked working on the paper, about her new home, about buildings, birds, and trees. About anything that moved or struck her fancy, about life. It reminded me of a rambling mood my mother had been in once, when everything around her interested and excited her and there was so much to say she could scarcely get the words out in their proper order. The mood came not long after she'd told me that hating the thought of dying paradoxically made her feel like killing herself, so she had to stop hating the thought of death in order to live a little longer and not hurt herself. But I did not want to think of Jewel as that sick. I did not want to picture her up there in the crowded sky above Los Angeles. It *could* just have been that getting away from Teddy had opened up her perceptions, made her interested in everything.

I decided to send her the rings we'd seen in the arroyo, as a surprise present. Mark drove with me down there. We'd gotten a late start because of a job he'd had that day, and it was getting uncomfortably late when we arrived. We slipped down the hillside, through some fairly thick brush. We wanted to avoid walking on any main paths and running into anyone.

It was easy to find the box this time. But when we opened it, the rings were gone and in their place was a slip of paper that said simply "Jewel, July 2052."

"She must have come back," said Mark.

I held the box, unsure what to do next. Then: "Do you have a pen?" I asked. I wrote "Francie and Mark" on a slip of paper. After a moment, I added "In Love, August 2052."

It was getting dark, though pale light dotted the clearing. Mark took off a bracelet and stuck it in the box. The bracelet was the first thing he'd ever bought with his own money after he'd moved out of the house at age fourteen. I took out my rocks and twig from my pouch, just to see them, and then returned them to the pouch and put the whole thing in the box for safekeeping until—whenever. We reburied everything and ascended the incline. The last sunlight had almost faded. Across the ravine a group of men threw a howling dog down below. The dog fell with an ugly thud. Farther along a roll of paper spiraled in the air and landed. It looked like a bandage on the earth, the way it lay. The men yelled at us, and someone shot a gun in the air. Another shot whistled to our side. Mark wadded up a piece of paper and threw it down. The men seemed to like that and moved on. Another group of people was walking on our side of the arroyo. They looked angrier, meaner even, than the ones who'd shot the gun off. Supposedly every night gangs roamed the arroyo, gangs who opposed the government, and gangs who supported it. We hurried to the car, but when we got there it was gone. I caught myself looking toward the sky for my parents. In the months to come, I knew, the sky would get even more crowded, and the dirt in the sky would start to look like dried blood.

"How will we get home?" I said. Several men ran toward us, yelling. We held hands and rushed back toward the arroyo to hide, slipping down into the thick brush. A branch ripped my cheek.

During the night as blood dried on my face, I heard the police chase away the crowds. Then someone dumped trash into the arroyo, the stench filling the air. All night I heard the dog howling in agony. My heart broke with every howl. Mark did not let go of my hand, and I don't think he slept all night. Los Angeles was the only home either of us had ever known, and maybe this would be the only love we would ever know. For those reasons, I knew I would never leave Los Angeles.

I could not.

CALIFORNIA FICTION

California Fiction titles are selected for their literary merit and for their illumination of California history and culture.

The Ford by Mary Austin	0-520-20757-2
Disobedience by Michael Drinkard	0-520-20683-5
Skin Deep by Guy Garcia	0-520-20836-6
Fat City by Leonard Gardner	0-520-20657-6
Continental Drift by James D. Houston	0-520-20713-0
In the Heart of the Valley of Love by Cynthia Kadohata	0-520-20728-9
Golden Days by Carolyn See	0-520-20673-8
Oil! by Upton Sinclair	0-520-20727-0
Who Is Angelina? by Al Young	0-520-20712-2

Forthcoming titles:

Thieves' Market by A. I. Bezzerides
Chez Chance by Jay Gummerman
The Vineyard by Idwal Jones
Bright Web in the Darkness by Alexander Saxton

Miriam Berkley

Cynthia Kadohata is the author of the novels *The Floating World* and *The Glass Mountains;* her screenplay for *The Floating World* has been optioned for a film by Kayo Hatta. Her short stories have appeared in *The New Yorker* and *Grand Street*. She is the recipient of a 1996 Chesterfield Screenwriting Fellowship and a 1991 Whiting Writers Fellowship and lives in Los Angeles.